The Treasure of Barracuda

Original title: El tesoro de Barracuda

© Llanos Campos, 2014

© Júlia Sardà, 2014

© Ediciones SM, 2014

English translation Copyright © 2016 by Little Pickle Press, Inc.

· English edition published by arrangement with Ediciones SM through
Sylvia Hayse Literary Agency LLC

All rights reserved.

Library of Congress Cataloging-in Publication Data is available.
Library of Congress Catalog Card Number on file.

Manufactured in the United States of America

10 9 8 7 6 5 4 3 2 1

ISBN 978-1-939775-14-6

Little Pickle Press, Inc.

3701 Sacramento Street #494

San Francisco, CA 94118 US

Please visit us at www.bigdillstories.com

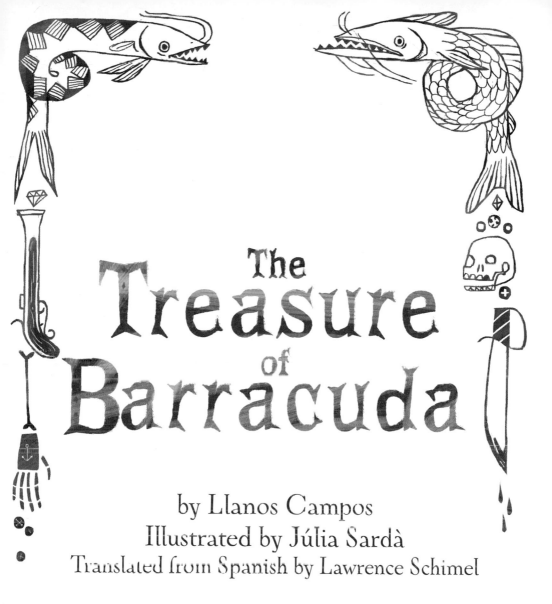

The Treasure of Barracuda

by Llanos Campos
Illustrated by Júlia Sardà
Translated from Spanish by Lawrence Schimel

BIG DILL STORIES

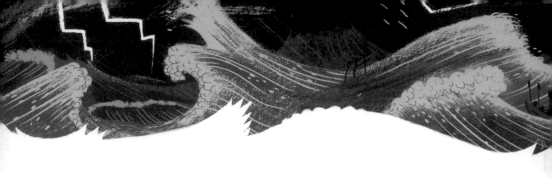

I'm going to tell you a story that I'm sure will seem incredible in many places. I know this, and it's not surprising because it's a story full of journeys to the end of the world, of winds that drive the bravest of men mad, of lost islands, and of sleepless nights beneath millions of stars. If I hadn't seen it with my own eyes, if I hadn't walked there with my own feet, it would seem incredible to me, too.

I can assure you, though, that what you are going to read is completely true. As true as the sea is salty and the sky is blue, and that the blackest eyes I've ever seen were those of an old woman named Dora, in Barbados. You don't yet know me, but you'll learn that I never, ever lie. And it's not because my parents taught me to behave this way (I never knew them), but because I've learned, after dealing with liars of all sorts, that lies bring problems for only one person: the one who speaks the lie. Believe me, you'll never get anywhere through a lie, no matter how good it seems to you. Sooner or later, someone will turn up who knows the truth, and then you'll have so many problems that you'll wish you had kept your mouth shut.

But let's leave the lessons for later. For now, I just want to give you a warning: if you come along with me, you'll need to be attentive and clever because we're going to visit dangerous places where you'll meet some people I wouldn't recommend meeting. I will guide you on the journey, and it's best if you heed me because, where we're going, mistakes can be quite costly, and there are no second chances.

To begin, I'll give you two pieces of advice that will serve you anywhere you go: one, never sit in a tavern with your back to the door; and two, when you're introduced to someone new, never open your mouth first. It's better to let the other person speak for a while until they no longer know what to say. Then an uncomfortable silence takes place, and just after it, if you manage to remain quiet a little longer, the other person will tell you something important, some secret that you can use later. This is because pirates hate silence. They're quarrelsome and noisy sorts, and they don't like to think too much.

Because (did I forget to say so earlier?) this is a story about pirates—with their ships, their eye patches, their wooden legs, and their hidden treasures.

I know, I know! You're going to tell me that you've already heard this story a thousand times, but I can assure you that you haven't. This will be, I promise, the strangest story of pirates you'll ever hear, even if you were to live a thousand years and travel to the last port of the Caribbean, listening to everyone who had something to say. I swear on it.

There was never a captain like Barracuda, there was never another adventure like ours, and no one could ever tell it better than I, who was there since the beginning.

The beginning…Yes…All this began…just like this…

"Blasted freshwater fishermen! And you call yourselves pirates?" Captain Barracuda shouted from the bridge. "I swear I'll hang anyone who abandons his station from the mizzen!"

The entire crew of the *Southern Cross* was terrified and shook in their boots. Barracuda was the pirate most feared by other pirates. Clever and merciless, he boasted of having no friends. His face was crisscrossed with scars. His left hand was missing, and in its place was an enormous, rusty hook. No one ever dared to ask him how he had lost it, so there were many legends about the matter.

"But, Captain…," Nuño, an old Spaniard who had sailed the Seven Seas, dared to say. "We've been sailing for ten days with no sign of the wretched island of Kopra. The men doubt if it really exists. Perhaps we should turn around…"

The pirates began shouting, protesting, and cursing in Spanish, Portuguese, Dutch, and English. So much swearing in so many languages that it's impossible for me to write it all down here.

"By all the devils of the sea," Barracuda roared, banging the ship's helm with his hook. "If you lot don't stop whining, I'll send you to swim with the sharks! I tell you that the island exists! And that it's there, right in front of your dirty noses! This ship will reach Kopra, even if I have to sail it alone! Whoever doesn't want to go can swim back to Maracaibo! I won't tolerate a mutiny on board!"

At that moment, Two Molars shouted from the crow's nest: "Land ahoy! To port! Yes! Land!"

For a moment, there was such a silence that you could have heard a cockroach scuttling.

"To your places, you slimy sardines," shouted Captain Barracuda. And as if they had gone mad, the pirates began running from one end of the deck to the other.

Among the pirates, a young one with a face full of freckles, green eyes, and a head full of red curls tugged on the cords that released the sails. That was me, Sparks. I was eleven-years-old and had been part of this crew since I was eight. Nuño had found me in a port on Española Island, where I'd been abandoned to my luck at some point I can't remember, and the other pirates had let me stay. At first, I gutted fish, helped in the kitchen, and swabbed the deck. Without complaining. That's why, finally, those men began to treat me with something like affection (pirate affection, you understand: knocks on the head, tugs at the ear, and slaps on the back). Little by little, they were willing to teach me things about the pirate profession. No one knows my name from before; even I don't remember it. So they called me Sparks (because of my red hair), and nothing more was said about the matter. So, if you suddenly read "we disembarked" or "we entered into battle," don't think that I'm exaggerating or lying. I was there.

But let's not get distracted from the story. We approached the island of Kopra. It was, as Barracuda had told us, barely a small pile of sand in the middle of the sea. We brought the ship in until the keel scraped the sandy bottom and then we lowered the boats. In them, piled together like the hairs of a beard, we rowed to the beach. Fifty-three pirates disembarked on that little island, and it was so crowded, it was fit to bursting. And if you tripped, there wasn't even room to fall. The captain commanded us to encircle the island and to stand in knee-deep water. So that's what we did. Then, Barracuda started counting off giant strides: two to the south, ten to the east, five to the north, two complete somersaults over his left shoulder, and two leaps backward on one leg.

Boasnovas, also called One-Eyed because, well, he had only one eye, was tempted to laugh, but he controlled himself. It wasn't time for jokes.

"Here it is!" Barracuda said, using his hook to mark an X in the sand. "Right here! Start digging!"

We took turns digging. While two dug, another two pushed the sand excavated from the hole to the sea. The rest of us stood looking on from the water's edge. It was such a small area; no one else could fit on the island. No one thought that such a tiny island could be so deep, but it took seven turns of two men digging

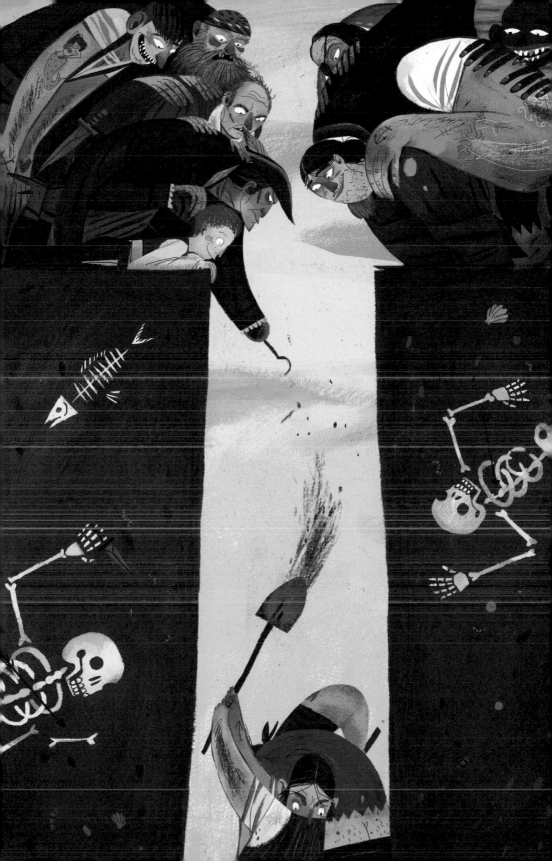

until, finally, one of the shovels hit something solid. It then took five pirates to pull it out of the hole.

It was an enormous black chest and as heavy as if the entire Dutch Antilles was inside it. Fifty-two pairs of eyes (plus Boasnovas's single eye) were fixated on it. If Barracuda was telling the truth (and nobody had ever caught him in a lie), then on that day all those pirates had just become filthy rich, so rich that they could leave behind a life of wandering the seas, if that's what they wanted. Because inside that dark wooden box was the famous treasure of Phineas Krane, the oldest pirate to have sailed the South Seas. And it was buried there because, as everyone knew, Phineas Krane died while boarding a Dutch vessel, right as he retired to enjoy his old age. Many had searched for the treasure since then, but only clever Barracuda had believed an old man who, in jail on the island of Tortuga, shouted at all hours that he knew exactly where Krane's treasure was.

"Fry me in pig fat!" Nuño the Spaniard exclaimed, with a smile that stretched from ear to ear. "He told the truth! That crazy old codger from Tortuga told the truth! Phineas Krane's treasure!"

A monumental ruckus erupted. Everyone cheered loudly for Barracuda, crying "Hurrah!" and "Bravo!" Then, the captain, using his hook as a lever, busted the lock on the coffer and lifted the heavy lid. The hinges let loose a rusty squeal.

If you had been there at that moment, you would have seen the most surprised group of pirates in the world, standing with their mouths and eyes opened wider than you would ever think was possible. Fifty-three defrauded pirates, that's what you would have seen. Because there, in the bottom of the enormous chest, was…a book! That was it! Phineas' treasure was a blasted book!

"Does anyone know how to read?" One-Legged Jack asked in a low voice.

We looked at one another.

"Well…I…a little," old Two Molars answered, and he picked up the book. He stared at it so intently; it looked as if his eyes were going to pop out. He read out loud in fits and starts: "My…Li-uf…as a…Pi…Pi…rate. by Phi…Phineas John… Johnson…Kra…ne."

By that point, Barracuda was as red as a chili pepper. "A book?

Years searching for a wretched book?" Barracuda screamed. The buttons of his jacket were ready to explode.

"Yes, Captain, but a book written by *him*," Nuño whispered. "They say there are writers who get rich that way…"

Then, Barracuda suffered a complete breakdown. He began to run like a madman, almost without moving from where he was, since as I've already explained, it was a minuscule island. With knees pumping high and arms flailing, he looked like he was being attacked by thousands of invisible ants. The crew, staring in disbelief, either cried about the treasure or laughed hysterically at the captain's antics.

11

The journey back to Maracaibo was terrible. We didn't dare open our mouths. It was the most silent crossing that had ever taken place on board a pirate ship, which is a noisy place, even at night. Because (let me tell you what almost no book ever reveals) pirates snore like mad. It's true! If you manage to sleep an entire night through while surrounded by these men, I assure you that you'd be able to sleep even inside the entrails of an active volcano.

But that's how the *Southern Cross* sailed—as if the entire crew had disappeared or died. It was almost funny to see men as large as mountains walking with care, almost on tiptoe, to avoid making the slightest noise on deck. For John the Whale, it was difficult to be stealthy; after all, he weighed one-hundred-and-fifty kilos and was more than two meters tall. So, he earned aggravated scoldings and slaps on the head from the other pirates.

The Barracuda was livid, and the pirates were terrified of his wrath. For an entire week after the Kopra debacle, the captain was holed up in his cabin, pacing back and forth and cursing in Turkish (his mother tongue, which he seldom used). Boasnovas, who was the cook as well as the artilleryman, delivered the captain his food. With a knot in his throat, Boasnovas opened the door just a bit, left the plate on the floor, and then quickly shut the door. Like what one does with a wild beast. A terrible silence ensued for a few days in the captain's quarters. Then one day, without warning, Barracuda finally emerged on deck carrying a mountain of plates.

"What the devil is going on here? Lousy lazybones! We should have reached Maracaibo a day ago! Nuño? Where's Nuño?"

The pirates pointed at the Spaniard, who, at that precise moment, was coming up from the hold. Nuño froze in place, holding the cord for which he had been searching.

"What…What's the matter?" he asked, nervously looking at his companions.

"The matter is that no one here does any work the moment I turn my back," Barracuda said, angrily lowering the tone of his voice. "The matter is that we're a day and a half late! That's what's the matter!"

"But, Captain…There's no wind and…"

"Excuses! That's the only thing you lot know how to do—make excuses! If there's no wind, then blow. I want to reach Maracaibo as soon as possible." He took a step and smashed some of the plates. "Someone clean up this mess!"

Barracuda returned to his cabin and slammed the door. The sun began to set, and then, perhaps not wanting to oppose the captain any longer, the wind, at last, began to blow and fill the sails. The ship picked up speed. Gathered in the prow, the men whispered to one another, trying to figure out Barracuda's plans. I was there, and I can say that no one correctly guessed what he

was going to do. Nobody knew why he was in such a hurry all of a sudden. For years, the captain had searched for Phineas Krane's treasure without rest. He intentionally had himself arrested in Tortuga to extract information from that old prisoner. Barracuda had heard about the crazy old guy, by chance, while in San Juan. Many of the *Southern Cross* pirates had followed Barracuda for many years because of his blind faith that he'd find Krane's lost treasure.

And now, those men were heading full tilt back to Maracaibo, with no plans beyond docking at the port and drinking jugs of rum. They were beyond disoriented. When at last we saw the lights of the port, it was late at night. Barracuda, as if someone had warned him, emerged from his cabin and in two strides, climbed to the bridge, grabbed the helm, and directed the docking maneuvers.

The piers were empty, and in the distance, in the city, one could faintly hear a pair of drunks fighting and a dog barking. As always, John the Whale leaped to the ground with breathtaking agility for someone his size and tied the rope to the prow. The pirates were ready to trod firm ground, after almost twenty days of bouncing around like crickets in a box.

But when the first man placed a foot on the gangplank to disembark, Barracuda spoke at last. He grabbed onto the helm and said in a loud and clear voice, "Good!" And with just that word, everyone froze in place and turned to look at the bridge. "This crew is dissolved. From this moment, I free you of your commitment to me. You can go and make a laughingstock of me; I won't reproach you. I have just one more thing to say: may that scurvy-livered Phineas rot in a cesspool of monkey slime! And now you can go."

All those pirates, coming from many different places, with different histories, and different ways of thinking, all remained equally stupefied. And all must have thought the same thing I did: "So what am I supposed to do from now on?" Nuño looked at Two Molars, Two Molars looked at Boasnovas, and Boasnovas looked at Erik the Belgian.

John the Whale, who climbed back on board at that precise moment, saw their faces and asked, "What's going on?"

"We've been thrown out," the Belgian said in a weak voice. He was a strong, tall guy and bald but (almost as if to compensate) with an enormous red mustache.

"Who's thrown us out? Where are they throwing us?" the Whale stuttered.

"Into the street," Boasnovas answered. "Onto solid ground. We're no longer the crew of the *Southern Cross*."

A collective sigh went up, and everyone sagged their shoulders in defeat. But the Whale still didn't understand.

"But, what have we done? What did we do wrong?"

"It's because of the treasure," said Malik, who was from Mali. "Because we didn't find it."

"But we did find it! Didn't we? It was just where Barracuda had said it was."

"I told you lot to get off of my ship," Barracuda bellowed, and in the bat of an eye, we were standing on the pier.

III

Three of the strangest of days went by. Fifty-two pirates wandered aimlessly around Maracaibo, without any appetite or thirst; we were in shock. Barracuda spent those three days cloistered in the English Inn, without seeing anyone. He went to the inn the night we landed and asked the inn's bookkeeper to write a note. Barracuda stuck it on the door and then went up to his room without saying a word. The paper read:

Full crew sought.
Offered: food and part of the booty, as usual.
No mangy curs nor big mouths accepted.
Candidates should present themselves on Saturday
morning in front of the Southern Cross,
on the western pier.

The announcement was at once the gossip of the entire city. Although, I will tell you that the poor bookkeeper had to read the sign to so many illiterate pirates that he almost tore it down and ate it. Many thought that the captain had fired us because of a mutiny. Others claimed that we had found Krane's treasure and that we were going to abandon pirating. Some heathens even tried to rob Malik in the Tavern of the Red Lady, but they instead treated him to dinner once they discovered he didn't have a single escudo on him.

A pirate can be a friend and also an enemy, according to circumstances; it's nothing personal. I don't know if the crew said anything in Maracaibo, but I know that Nuño and I didn't say anything to anyone about Kopra. And John the Whale didn't say anything because he was with us those days, and he was unable to form a single word as if he had suddenly become an orphan—an enormous and silent orphan.

I must say, for those who don't know it, Maracaibo is a foul hole where the worst of the worst come to rest: thieves, swindlers, assassins, and traitors of all kinds. If you'd seen the things I've seen, you'd prefer to be lost in a jungle full of hungry tigers rather than to be on the streets of Maracaibo. That's why, as soon as we saw the captain's announcement, we three knew, without a doubt, what we were going to do. But what happened on Saturday morning was something that we could have never imagined.

I can still picture Captain Barracuda's face when he arrived early that day on the pier hoping to find a row of men ready to embark, but he found only the same pirates who had disembarked three days earlier! The entire crew was there—not one pirate missing—ready to head off wherever the wind would take us. No questions asked!

The captain was thunderstruck, and if he wondered how it was possible that no one else had shown up, he didn't say anything. But I think that when he saw Boasnovas' black eye, One-Legged Jack's split lip, and the other pirates' bruises, he understood that it hadn't been easy for us to get rid of the other candidates. He walked slowly, looking at us one by one. The Whale smiled at him, the Belgian cleared his throat, Malik saluted him like a soldier, and I didn't know what to do.

Only Nuño, the captain's right-hand man, took a step forward and, showing the notice he had torn from the door of the English

Inn, said, "Captain, we've come to enlist on the *Southern Cross*."

Barracuda was silent for just a few seconds, but it seemed like hours. "What is this? A joke?" he said at last.

"Hardly a joke," Nuño said, adjusting his vest. "We're presenting ourselves on the day and at the time indicated on this announcement."

Another eternal silence.

"That business about the treasure doesn't matter to us!" a voice called out from the back, and the captain tensed, clenching his teeth.

"What I mean to say is…That is, it's that…" Two Molars stammered, twisting what little hair hung from his head.

But he couldn't say anything more, so Nuño spoke again. "The sea is full of ships heavy with gold, and we'll have opportunities to capture them. We're pirates. We don't know how to do anything else. So it's obvious: you need men, and we need to sail. It's advantageous for everyone."

Anyone familiar with Barracuda knew that he was never content (or at least, he never seemed to be), and he never had a kind word for anyone. We didn't know how Barracuda would react to our proposition since we were dealing with one of the harshest pirates of the Caribbean's emerald waters.

And here's what happened: the captain climbed aboard, went to the bridge, and remained there, silent as a coat rack. And we pirates, standing there on land, didn't know what to do. That's how that man was!

Nuño, who knew Barracuda best, tentatively stepped onto the gangplank, like someone sticking a foot into a puddle of crocodiles. The wood creaked. Barracuda didn't move a muscle, and so Nuño shouted, "Let's set sail! Everyone to their stations! What are you waiting for, a map of the deck?"

And we, after looking at one another, ran on board as if we had rehearsed it, without tripping or even bumping into one another, straight to our places. The Whale released the moorings, and other pirates pulled on the riggings and loosened the sailcloths. No one noticed that Two Molars had climbed onto the ship with a suspicious package under his arm, just as no one had noticed that he had disembarked with it three days earlier. But don't you forget it because it's important. It's a fact that, if he hadn't done it, this story wouldn't have taken place. Because without any of us the wiser, Phineas Krane's book had disembarked and re-embarked with Two Molars.

We set sail for Española, an island on the main route of ships returning to Europe loaded with gold and precious stones. And, you might recall, the island on which I had been abandoned years ago. It was a good place for us to get to work and practice our primary trade: boarding and looting ships.

We were in good spirits, except for Barracuda, who spent the nights pacing the deck like a lost soul. It was going to be difficult for him to forget that he had wasted six years of his life searching for what he thought was a fabulous treasure and what had proven to be a disaster. For the rest of us, accustomed to the ebbs and flows of a pirate's life, it didn't seem too serious a setback, to tell the truth. We were pirates, after all—men who earned fortunes by day and lost them by night; men who went to bed rich and woke up dirt poor; and men who ate in a palace on Monday and wallowed in a dungeon on Wednesday. Anything else would have surely bored a pirate.

Four days later, someone (I think it was One-Legged Jack) discovered Two Molars crouching under the pantry steps, reading by the light of a candle. Two Molars begged One-Legged Jack not to say anything. And it's not that Jack was a gossip or anything like that; he was a little Englishman with one wooden leg (a peg leg) who didn't talk much at all. But who would think that a secret could be kept in a floating shell full of men with nothing to do except look at one another for hours on end? And, thus, the next night, Two Molars had more of an audience than he might've desired.

We went down into the pantry, Erik the Belgian, Boasnovas, Jack, and myself (I carried a lighted candle). The Whale followed and tried to slip in with us, but, as I've already told you, it wasn't easy for him to pass unnoticed. His steps sounded like an elephant's as he came down the wooden stairs. As soon as Two Molars saw us, he hid something behind his back and began to shout and curse for us to leave and get some fresh air on deck. But, of course, we didn't go.

"What have you got there?" asked Erik the Belgian in a loud voice, making us all giggle.

"Don't shout," One-Legged Jack chided him. "Do you want everyone to come down here?"

"Come on, what have you got there?" Boasnovas repeated, trying to speak softly. "Sparks, lift up that light so we can see what it is!"

I lifted the candle, and Two Molars, who was a reasonable fellow, understood that he couldn't hide whatever it was for very long, being on a ship in the middle of the sea and with days and days ahead of us before landfall. So he gave in. Slowly, from behind his back, he pulled something rectangular wrapped in a dirty piece of cloth. He placed it on the floor and unwrapped it.

Our eyes nearly leaped from their sockets.

"Is it...the book of the treasure?" John the Whale asked.

"Phineas' book," Boasnovas exclaimed, softly.

"It didn't belong to anyone," Two Molars replied. "And nobody wanted it!"

"And what did you want it for?" the Whale asked him. "A book! Why, none of us can read!"

"A little bit," Two Molars muttered. "I said I could read, a little bit!"

"But...why do you want a book?" Erik asked as he turned the pages full of squiggles that none of us could understand.

"That's none of your business," Two Molars answered, snapping the book closed.

"What do you mean it isn't?" Boasnovas asked, his eye crossed. "This loot belongs to all of us...If it's worth something, you should tell us."

"It isn't worth anything! It's a souvenir, nothing more!" Two Molars said.

"A what?" the Whale whispered behind us. "Wasn't it a book?"

"Oh, shut up, you oaf!" Erik the Belgian answered. "It's French."

"The book?"

"No, Whale, no! The word! *Souvenir* is French; it means a memento."

"I don't understand anything...Why do we care if it's French?"

"Shut your big trap, Whale!" Boasnovas told him, losing his patience. "And you, Two Molars, explain why you wanted to bring Krane's book on board."

"Yeah, that's right!" Jack added. "It must be worth something since you kept it...and haven't breathed a word about it to the rest of us!"

"It's not worth a thing, I tell you," Two Molars shouted back. "Leave me alone already! It's...It's just...It's just that it names me!"

"That it what?" I asked, not understanding anything.

"It names me," said Two Molars. "I am in there, in this book! When I was flipping through it, I saw my name. I was curious to know what old Phineas had written about me. I was with him on the *Prince of Antigua,* a ship unlike anything you've ever seen. I sailed under his command for almost four years, before he set off for the Southern Seas, and I can tell you that he was smarter than the devil himself."

"You are in the book!" Boasnovas said, his mouth gaping, while his single eye ran across the pages. "Where? Tell me where it says 'Two Molars.'"

"It doesn't say that anywhere! I was younger then. Nobody called me that...It says my real name: Anton the Corsican."

"Anton?" we all said in chorus, and a little giggle escaped from John the Whale.

"Yes," the toothless old man said, staring us down. "Do you think I was born with these wrinkles and a mouth like this?"

"No, we're sure that you were born with fewer teeth than the two you have now," Boasnovas said, quietly laughing.

"Come on, Two Molars, read what it says about you," One-Legged Jack said, offering him the book.

Then, the man formerly known as Anton the Corsican took the enormous tome, opened his underpopulated mouth, and began to read in fits and starts. I will reproduce the text here without the many, overlong pauses Two Molars made as he read. I don't want to abuse your patience.

> *We sailed following the wake of a ship named The Lady of the Sea. We knew that she returned to Veracruz loaded with gold from the booty of Portobelo. We had gotten the tip thanks to the fact that Anton, a young lad born in Corsica who sailed with me, had managed to become friendly with a French merchant marine whom he had invited for a drink in a Miskito Cays' tavern. I had no doubt that the information was trustworthy because the clever Corsican speaks fluent French and because he could also spot a liar from across the room.*

When Two Molars finally finished reading, we looked at him with something resembling admiration. We had never known anyone whose name was in a book, immortalized in ink forever. At most, we had seen our faces drawn on some "Wanted" poster, with a sum listed below as a reward. Two Molars was so puffed up; I thought his boots would come unbuckled. But all this magic was undone by the Whale when he asked, "And what about me? Does it say something about me?"

"How is it going to say anything about you, Whale," Erik the Belgian said, rolling his eyes. "Let's see now, did you know Phineas Krane?"

"Me?"

"Yes, you!"

"Know Krane?"

"Yes!"

"Not me…"

"Well then, there you have it. How is he supposed to have written something about you, you big mackerel? He wrote a book about his life, about the people he knew! Why would he mention you?" Erik asked.

"I'm a pirate too…Maybe he mentions me." Now the Whale got a bit angry. "What do you know? You don't know how to read! There are lots of words there! Maybe one of them is 'John Tortichellobelloponte'!"

"What?" we all said in unison.

"Tortich-what?" I asked, unable to believe what I'd heard.

"Tortichellobelloponte," he repeated calmly. "My mother said my father was Italian."

"It doesn't matter," Boasnovas said, putting an end to the question. "Whatever you're called, it's not possible for you to appear in the book…Perhaps old Two Molars isn't even in there! Who knows if what he read aloud is actually in the book? He could tell us anything, taking advantage of us because we don't know how to read."

"That's absurd! What do I gain from lying to all of you?" asked Two Molars. "Besides, nobody asked you here. I was just fine here all on my own!"

"Then, this tells everything about Old Phineas' life," I said, really interested, picking up the heavy book for the first time. "Wow! It must be a fascinating story. They say he was as clever a pirate as anyone—one of those people who always knew how to be in the right place at the right time. And courageous! People still talk in awe of the treasures he looted and the ships he captured."

"That's true, lad," One-Legged Jack agreed. "Nobody could hold a candle to him on the sea. Barracuda was still a babe when

Krane was already the scourge of these waters. Just to speak his name provoked such fear in some ports that they called him the Typhoon because after he came through, nobody remained standing."

"I saw him once," Erik the Belgian said. "In Martinique. He was with men who, most likely, were from the Orient. Back then, nobody had seen many Chinese around here, so they immediately attracted attention. Krane was buying black powder. After that, he captured more than fourteen ships. I served Olaf the Magician back then. Maybe Krane remembered me in the book. We ate in the same place…It would have been impossible to overlook us: a table full of noisy blonds and redheads!"

"Don't be ridiculous, Erik!" interrupted Nuño, who had followed us down. "You're nothing more than a Northern brute like thousands of others. Now I, on the hand, spent an entire night with him, in jail in Belize. The next morning, his crew freed him, but we had time for a long, extended talk. I am sure that's in his book. We had a lot of laughs."

"Two Molars!" I suddenly cried out, without knowing why. "Teach me to read!"

"To read?" John the Whale repeated, staring at me as if I were some strange creature that crawled out from the sea. "Why would you ever want to do something so difficult?"

"Why, to know what it says here!" I answered, running my finger across the etchings on the cover of the book. "The life of Phineas Krane! Can you imagine? With all the things he did, the adventures he had, and the treasures he won! It must be an incredible story to listen to! And it's all here, in his own voice… Well, in his own hand, at any rate! Teach me!" I insisted.

"No! No…" Two Molars stuttered. "I wouldn't know…It's hard enough for me to recognize some letters…I go very slowly."

"We're in no rush," Boasnovas said. "We're trapped on this boat for days, with nothing to do but watch our toenails grow. The boy's right! Perhaps in this book are the clues to find the many treasures Krane won!"

"What he's saying is not all foolishness," Nuño said, rubbing his goatee. "Maybe we really did find a treasure in Kopra…I want to learn how to read with you, Sparks!"

"Me, too!" Jack and Boasnovas said, almost at the same time.

"I don't think I could," John the Whale sighed beside us.

"I've been banged on the head so often that I wouldn't know how to learn…"

"That doesn't matter," I said to encourage him. "You've got a really hard skull; I'm sure your brain is safe."

"Then it's decided," Nuño said, standing up. "We'll meet here every night at eight, before dinner. And we'll have a lesson in reading."

"My goodness!" Erik the Belgian exclaimed. "I've never gone to a class in my life! But I am not going to be left out of this. If it says something important there, I want to read it with my own eyes."

"But…But I…" Two Molars blubbered, his eyes as round as saucers. "I don't know if…"

"You'll do it very well," Nuño decided. "And we will all pay attention to you, I promise. But be careful." His tone became serious. "Don't even think of teaching us badly on purpose, so we understand things backward, you understand?"

"I swear I wouldn't know how to do that, Nuño. I'll do… I'll do what I can, my comrades," said Two Molars solemnly.

He didn't yet know it, but this was going to be one of the most difficult things he'd ever have to do in his life. On the first day, we were six students; on the second day, nine; and by the fourth day, the news had spread like a match in a powder keg, and then the entire crew was sitting on the pantry floor at eight on the dot. Everyone except Barracuda, who watched his crew disappear as soon as the sun began to set. But he didn't ask anything; it wouldn't do for it to look like he cared about the private lives of his men. He wasn't that kind of captain.

I have never gone to school—not one single day—but I know that no professor has endured students like these: pirates with scars and tattoos, blackened teeth, wearing torn and stinking clothes, and armed with knives in their belts. No one, I can assure you, has ever attended a class like ours. We pirates were all seated in the pantry of the *Southern Cross*, making more grimaces than a troop of monkeys. Between the ones who couldn't see very well, those who couldn't speak well, and those who didn't hear well, Two Molars had the most difficult job in the world. It was like trying to teach a flock of ducks how to sew.

And Two Molars wasn't what one would call a good teacher although the poor man did the best he could. Sometimes he would grab his head as if he were afraid it might come unscrewed from his neck and fly up into the air. We asked him everything at the same time, and he tried to remember what little he knew. I think that sometimes he even invented things, just so we would leave him in peace.

He began by teaching us the letters, and it seemed incredible to us that there were so many of them. John the Whale insisted that he didn't use more than half of them when he talked, and it didn't matter that we tried to convince him otherwise; he was as stubborn as a mule. Of course, that was nothing compared to when we began to put letters together to make words. That was interminable. Because if it was difficult to know how they sounded two by two, as soon as we made bundles of three letters, that really put a spanner in the works! There we all were, opening our mouths, sticking our tongues out, making pouting faces, and rubbing our eyes. And, of course, sooner or later someone started to laugh and then you had a whole rumpus going on. What with "What are you laughing at?" and "Me? Nothing." and "I'll give you something to laugh about."…And then: a full-on brawl.

And on top of everything, Two Molars, as I've already mentioned, had an extremely limited knowledge of reading. Often, he got letters all mixed up, especially the lowercase "b" and "d" which look so similar. So instead of saying "drown" he read "brown."

That's why nobody understood what Erik the Belgian meant when, after much effort and turning blue from nerves, he read: "They made him walk the plank and watched him 'brown.'" He got really mad when One-Legged Jack asked him, "What are you talking about, you oaf? What does it matter if he got a tan?"

"What do you want from me?" Erik replied. "I didn't write it! I just read what's there!"

"He reads it, he says! You're inventing it!" yelled Jack.

"Listen, Jack, don't mess with me, or you're going to have to read without teeth! Let's see then how you'll manage to say 'skirmish' or 'weigh anchors'!"

There were thousands of arguments like that. Every day we had more questions than Two Molars had answers, even when he invented the answers. As soon as we picked up some momentum with our learning, something else hit us: capital and lowercase letters and accents. And just as things seemed clearer, here came the B and the V, the G and the H.

"Well, that's about enough!" Boasnovas declared one day, knocking the book off the table with a huge swipe of his hands. "You're mocking us! Why the devil are 'said' and 'paid' pronounced differently if they're spelled the same? You're fooling us, you crazed Corsican!"

"Do you want us to look like idiots?" John the Whale asked.

"Yeah! What he said!" the Belgian joined the protest. "You want to be the only one who reads well so that you don't have to share the secrets of Phineas' book with us!"

"That's right!" the rest chorused in protest.

Anton the Corsican, now known on the *Southern Cross* as Two Molars, was about to cause a mutiny of students on board. You had to have lived it to believe it! So he stood up, took the book, and climbed the steps two by two. Before he closed the trapdoor of the deck, he said, "That's it! I told you I didn't know how to teach anyone how to read! I don't have to stand for this! Find yourselves some other fool who'll put up with you!"

And he slammed the trapdoor shut.

First, we all got mad, of course. And then we didn't know what to do.

The next day, the crew was in a foul mood, Two Molars worse than everyone. He spent all day at his watch station atop the highest mast, even though we were sailing on the open sea with nothing to see but water, more water, and yet more water. He was as mad as a wet hen.

Days passed with many glances exchanged but few words spoken. Our professor stayed angry. But something else began to happen to the rest of us. Suddenly, we realized that above the door to Barracuda's chambers, someone had written "Captain;" that on the barrels of rum it really did say "Rum;" and not just that, but someone had also written "from Puerto Rico." And, most importantly, we could put the barrels together in the hold because now we could distinguish barrels that contained rum from those that held gunpowder because those barrels read "Gunpowder"!

Of course, not all of the news was good news. Let One-Legged Jack tell you: he'd been convinced that an Amazonian shaman had tattooed on his right arm, under a drawing of a jaguar, the words "Strength and Fierceness," until he could read for himself that it read "Pretty Kitty." You don't want to know the jokes that were made after that. He even thought of cutting his arm off, but we convinced him that he was already missing one leg, and to cut off an arm now would be losing too many body parts for a single lifetime.

And that's how things were when we reached Española. And, you have to believe me, it was as if we were visiting it for the first time. We walked through the streets open-mouthed and overwhelmed. We realized that so many words were all over the place—so many things to read and so much information we were unaware of before. The street names were curious to us. We didn't know that the jail was on "Calvary Street" or that the livestock market was on "The Street of the Portuguese." You can't believe how proud Boasnovas was about that! I know it wasn't named for him, but what did it matter? Who wanted to take away his joy for no reason?

And so we wandered, like children in a candy store, elbowing one another and competing to see which of us could read the signs of the stores or the names of the bottles first. And we were astonished when John the Whale pointed out a poster which read "Vorbidden" spelled just like that. "With a V instead of an F!" he shouted. We could have never appreciated a joke like this before. The big lunk stood there, crying tears of laughter before the incredulous gaze of the poor shopkeeper who didn't know the difference between a V and an F. So John asked the shopkeeper for a piece of chalk and corrected the spelling, under the gaze of a proud Two Molars.

That's the good thing about reading: once you start, there's no stopping you! Words, once you reach that pivotal moment, seem to come together and everything appears to be clear and simple. You might suddenly see a word whose meaning you don't know, but, incredibly, you're still able to read it. You see the word "medic" written and, of course, you don't know what it means. But now you can ask: "Hey, what's a medic?" And thus, you learn that it's another way of saying doctor. At first, it seems like magic.

In the Tavern of the Golden Hand, for the first time ever, we asked to see the menu so that we could choose what we wanted to eat. We discovered that chicken could be cooked eight different ways and pork, on the other hand, in only five; that almost everything came with potatoes; and that fish was much cheaper than meat. With so much information on the menu, it took us over one hour to order our meal! So many decisions!

We were oblivious that we were attracting attention, but we should have known better. Here we were, a group of pirates passing the menu to one another and reading aloud what it said: "No spitting at the tables;" "Weapons must be left with the tavern keeper during the meal;" or "Don't trust, now or ever." Barracuda, seated with Nuño on the other side of the tavern's enormous room, watched us with his famous blank-face stare. Nuño, as he later told us, neither could nor wished to lie to him, so, when Barracuda asked him, he told the captain about the reading lessons and Phineas Krane's book. If the captain was surprised, he didn't say, and nobody noticed anything. He merely told Nuño to order another pitcher of beer and dove back into his dark thoughts, a place from which no one could budge him— not even with a shot from a cannon!

After eating our fill, we ordered jugs of rum and grog as if we were at a wedding. We kept filling Two Molars' glass to see if we could get him to forget about our complaints and to forgive us. The thing is, in case you didn't know, pirates never ask for forgiveness, even if they accidentally fall to their knees with their hands clasped together. At most, they'll give you a knock on the skull or an elbow to the ribs, although most common is for them to offer you something to drink, for nobody to say anything, and for the matter to be forgotten.

Of course (let me say this so that everything is clear), I didn't drink anything other than water. I was eleven-years-old, and my crewmates would have shaved my head bald if they'd caught me sticking my jaw near a jug of alcohol of any kind. "Children don't drink, or they'll not grow," they told me all the time; although it would never have even occurred to me to try those foul-smelling concoctions. That night, no one drank much, incredibly. They were occupied enough reading the bottles and debating whether the beers from the continent were better than those from the islands, or if the drinks that said "spirits" on the bottles had a ghost inside.

Back on the *Southern Cross*, we found ourselves with the problem of how fifty-two pirates were going to read a single book. First, we thought we'd read it aloud by turns, but that didn't work. Between "You read too slowly" and "I can't understand you with that thick Belgian accent," not to mention "We can't hear if you read without teeth" or "I'm too embarrassed...." You guessed it: more fights, more heads bashed, more ruckus. So we decided to pass the book from person to person in turns. There were a lot of us; by the time it was your turn again, you couldn't recall what you had already read, but it was the only way for us to have peace on board.

With this agreement in place, and controlling the times with a small hourglass, the following days passed calmly. Barracuda watched us from time to time and seemed to be making mental notes about something. That made me feel uneasy; the captain was unpredictable, and his surprises could be good... or the exact opposite.

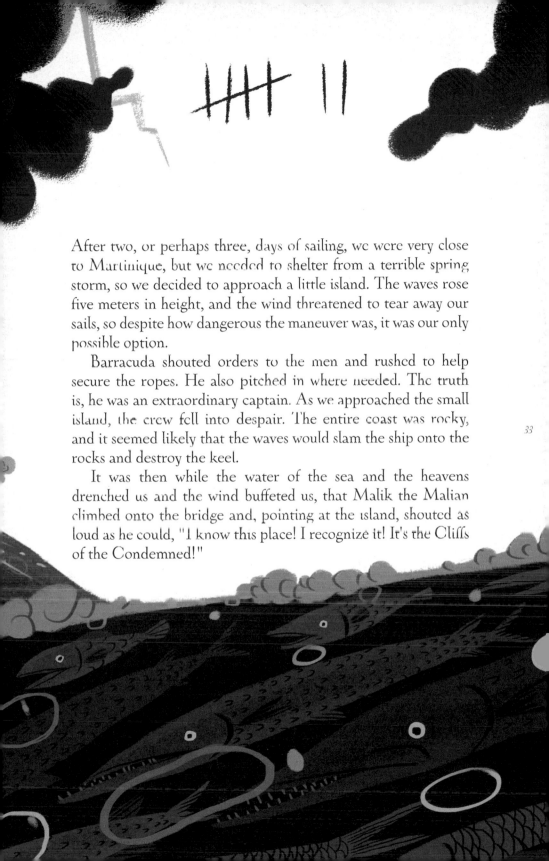

After two, or perhaps three, days of sailing, we were very close to Martinique, but we needed to shelter from a terrible spring storm, so we decided to approach a little island. The waves rose five meters in height, and the wind threatened to tear away our sails, so despite how dangerous the maneuver was, it was our only possible option.

Barracuda shouted orders to the men and rushed to help secure the ropes. He also pitched in where needed. The truth is, he was an extraordinary captain. As we approached the small island, the crew fell into despair. The entire coast was rocky, and it seemed likely that the waves would slam the ship onto the rocks and destroy the keel.

It was then while the water of the sea and the heavens drenched us and the wind buffeted us, that Malik the Malian climbed onto the bridge and, pointing at the island, shouted as loud as he could, "I know this place! I recognize it! It's the Cliffs of the Condemned!"

"What are you talking about, Malik?" Erik yelled. "Are you crazy? This is just some miserable little rock in the middle of the sea. I doubt that anyone has even bothered to give it a name!"

"Phineas did!" Malik shouted. "It's in the book! Didn't anyone else reach Chapter Seven?" Then he pointed at the island again. "Look there! Those are the Two Brothers!"

We looked to where he was pointing, and we saw, up high and silhouetted against the gray sky, two enormous pointy rocks towering above the treeline.

"The book describes this very place," Malik explained. "We need to go around the island to reach the north face."

"And why would we need to do that?" Barracuda spat. "This place is a wretched ship trap! We should pull away now and try to find some other port!"

"Captain, the storm is growing by the minute," Nuño interrupted. "I don't think we can reach Barbados."

"That won't be necessary, Nuño!" Malik insisted. "Captain, trust me! I know that to the north, there is a cove that's deep enough for this ship. Krane's book describes it in full detail!"

Barracuda stared at Malik as if he were trying to count the hairs in his eyebrows. Two enormous thunderclaps shook the ship, and lightning bolts streaked across the sky from west to east and then back again. Then, the captain's voice rang out above the storm: "Nuño, full to port! Change course to the north!"

Barracuda grabbed Malik by the shirt and yanked him forward until Malik's nose was almost touching the captain's scruffy beard. "And you, you better pray that that blasted book is correct! If I lose this ship, you'll never find a hole deep enough to hide in from me, you water rat!"

"You won't lose it, Captain!" Malik assured him and then ran toward Nuño to indicate the course.

As we turned north, with the *Southern Cross* creaking and popping like an old bed, the gale winds grew even stronger.

"There!" Malik shouted. "It's there! Between those two little inlets! My God, it's just as the book describes!"

Nobody saw an opening in the coastline, but, without time to doubt any further, we hurried to steer the ship to where he indicated. And to the relief and surprise of everyone…there it was! The ship, little by little, made its way through a narrow canal and suddenly entered a broad and deep cove. It was as if we had entered *inside* the little island itself. The wind abated, and the waters grew calm.

The pirates remained as open-mouthed as they were relieved. They had sailed by this island hundreds of times and had never suspected that this refuge existed. We dropped anchor in the middle of that marina, and everything was calm.

"Well blow me over!" Erik the Belgian said. "It's a miracle! But what is this place? I've never heard a peep about it...It's completely hidden from the sea."

"Phineas knew about it," Jack said with sincere admiration. "That's why he often said he was able to disappear on the sea. I don't think anyone else knew about this little hideaway. Did you?" he asked Two Molars, who answered back, "Of course not! He must have found it after I left his crew."

We spent all night talking nonstop about Krane. We were thrilled to imagine what awaited us in his book.

We arrived in Barbados the next day. Before we disembarked, Barracuda admonished us to not breathe a word about the hidden cove. The captain had a business meeting with an Italian fabrics merchant named Bruno. Many of the ships we captured had expensive-looking pearly fabrics and metallic-colored brocades, and Barracuda almost always sold them to Bruno.

After Malik's success with the refuge in the Cliffs of the Condemned, we decided to carry the book with us. This time, there were no tavern visits, no fistfights, no staying out celebrating until dawn. We spent the entire time reading by turns and taking notes on things that Phineas talked about in his book. Perhaps something else might be of use at some other moment, like what had happened with the hidden cove that had saved the *Southern Cross* and, as a consequence, all of us.

Everyone stared at us, but that was to be expected; no one had ever seen a group of pirates sitting on a beach, quiet as a tomb, passing a book from one to the other every ten minutes. We sat there, looking at the sea like happy shipwrecks. And when the pirate who was reading suddenly laughed or was surprised by something, others asked what it was and yet others said, "Don't say anything, I want to read it myself!" When we got hungry, we even decided that someone should go and buy provisions and bring them back for us to eat right there. Well, as you might imagine, that fell to me, although the Whale offered to help me.

Don't ridicule me! You couldn't carry enough food for all those hungry pirates by yourself either.

But what I really want to tell you about those days in Barbados happened a day and a half later.

As I've mentioned, Barracuda had an appointment with Bruno, the fabric merchant, in the Tavern of the Siamese Parrot. Nuño, the Whale, and I accompanied the captain. We pirates are brave, but we're not foolish, and anyone who's been at this for more than a month knows that you don't show up to a business meeting alone. It's not out of fear; it's because a wary pirate lives longer than a trusting one.

You might say (and you'd be right) that a child of eleven years is of little use, but I liked to be in the middle of everything. And you can thank me that I was there because that's why I can now tell this story with all the fullest details. Few things happened that I wasn't present to witness myself.

It would have been enough for Barracuda to take only John the Whale to the meeting. The Whale was a formidable figure, and most pirates from other crews gulped just on seeing him. If you had known him the way I did, you'd have realized that he was as good as he was big. He was always saving little kittens from palm trees and petting flea-infested dogs in the most wretched of hovels. He was a softie. But, without a doubt, he was a *big* softie. And in a fight, if it was necessary, he swung those huge fists of his with precision. But only when it was absolutely necessary.

So there we were, at the Tavern of the Siamese Parrot. We on one side of the table, and Bruno the Italian on the other side. Bruno was a handsome and slender sort who didn't look like a pirate (nor did he claim to be one) but who was more dangerous than many who wore a patch and a wooden leg. Bruno was a serious man, never one to joke. He was accompanied by an imposing Turk, whose face was split by an enormous scar and who wore a long dagger on his belt. Two others (possibly Frenchmen) also stood there but never said a word. They stared at us so intently; it looked like they wanted to engrave our faces on their memories.

The conversation was brief. Barracuda told Bruno what we had brought that might interest him, and the Italian named a price. Things might've ended there, with a "Here's your merchandise" and "Here's your money," but Bruno tried to be clever. First, to pay for the fabrics, he put a leather bag of coins on the table, and Nuño picked it up. Then, without anyone expecting it or asking for it, Bruno pulled out a document, placed it on the table, and told the captain to sign it.

"It's better to have things written down so that we all know what we've agreed to. If you place an X here, that'll be sufficient," said Bruno.

Barracuda looked at the paper, and then with greater scrutiny at Bruno, who smiled like a bride. I didn't realize that even though the handwriting was terribly messy, the Whale was reading the paper over my shoulder.

"Wait a minute!" the Whale said, pounding one of his meaty paws on the table.

Both Nuño and I jumped back, startled, but the captain didn't even blink. The Whale picked up the document and shook it under Bruno's nose.

"Do you think we're fools?" he asked. "The seas will dry up before Barracuda signs this trash!"

And then he read at a good pace:

37

> *The captain named Barracuda promises via this document to reserve all the merchandise he acquires on his journeys for Bruno Castilfierro. From this date forward, Mr. Castilfierro will have preference to choose whatever is of interest to him and to name the price.*

Barracuda smiled while he stared at Bruno; John the Whale crumpled the piece of paper, and, to the astonishment of all, swallowed it in a single gulp. That's what the big lunk was like; he loved to make big, theatrical gestures.

"Well, Castilfierro," the captain said very slowly. "Perhaps you thought it would be simple to trick me…Yes, you no doubt thought that. On the other hand, I don't know how you thought a miserable slip of paper could force me to do anything. We're pirates; papers don't matter to us, signatures don't matter to us; our word is enough. If I make a deal, I keep it. Anyone who knows me knows that this is true. And they also know that I never forgive a betrayal. Without exceptions, Italian…."

An uncomfortable silence followed, to say the least. The two Frenchmen stepped forward, and the Turk placed his hand on his

dagger and grunted like a trapped dog.

"Careful," I thought. "Don't let anyone do anything foolish at this moment."

Nuño put the leather bag of coins back on the table.

"We'll leave this here, gentlemen," Nuño said calmly. "There is no deal. Here is your money, and each of us will go our way."

"Come now, Barracuda!" the merchant protested. "Let's not get nervous. That money is yours. What are you going to want with all those fabrics? Are you going to have flowered sails on the *Southern Cross*? It was a misunderstanding and that's that."

Bruno looked at Barracuda, but the captain didn't open his mouth again. It was the Whale who spoke next.

"Misunderstandings, bah! You thought you were dealing with a bunch of ignorant pirates, but you've shot yourself in the foot!"

I elbowed him, and he fell quiet.

"There is no deal," Nuño repeated, chewing his words. "And no more discussion."

Barracuda stood up, glaring nonstop at Bruno. I'll tell you the truth, when he gets like this, the captain is frightening. Then Barracuda left the room without looking back.

We did just the opposite: we left walking backward, without taking our eyes off the four angry men at the table. Bruno stood with his fist clenched upon the table and with a face that looked so angry, it was almost funny. Of course, we had no idea that things wouldn't end there and that we would once again cross paths with Bruno Castilfierro.

Out on the street again, John the Whale was as happy as a child with new clothes.

"Did you see that, Sparks? I read it in one go!" The enormous pirate skipped around me like a little puppy wagging its tail. "I looked at the paper, and I said to myself: 'I know how to read this! I know all these letters!' Oh my! Did you see, Nuño? Did you see? I did it well, didn't I?"

"You did it wonderfully, Whale," Barracuda suddenly said from in front of us, without stopping or turning around.

Great big John was gobsmacked as if he'd just been struck by lightning. The captain, who had never said anything good about anyone, had just praised him! That night, without a doubt, the happiest pirate beneath the Caribbean stars was my good friend John the Whale!

The next day, still in the port of Barbados, the crew made us tell them again and again about the encounter with Bruno, the fabric merchant. Every time we reached the bit about the contract, I added some detail to make the tale more interesting, and the Whale laughed like a little kid.

Barracuda remained at the prow of the ship, thinking about who-knows-what. Suddenly he gave a shout:

"NUÑO!"

The Spaniard leaped to attention and hurried toward him. They spoke in low voices. Nuño was very surprised by something the captain said to him and shook his head no with vigor. Then he pointed to Two Molars and Erik the Belgian, both of whom became worried. And, since Barracuda seemed to insist, Nuño then pointed to the rest of us; we all became worried. After that, a silence ensued during which the two men stared at one another. Suddenly, Nuño shot away from the prow like a spring and headed over to us, muttering under his breath, "My rotten foul luck!"

"What did the captain want?" John the Whale asked, placing a hand on Nuño's shoulder to stop him.

Nuño stared at him.

"For me to teach him how to read!" And then he repeated, "My rotten foul luck!"

One-Legged Jack suddenly started to cackle. "Woo hoo!" he said, between giggles. "He's going to pull your head off! Explain diphthongs to him, Nuño!" He laughed even more. "Cheer up, my friends! Soon we'll have a vacancy for the post of second in command on this ship!"

Nuño kept walking and sat down in the stern, trying no doubt to invent a better excuse than the ones he had already given the captain to get out of this order.

"Leave him be," the Whale said. "He's got enough problems…"

"Nuño!" Barracuda shouted again from the prow. "Do I need to repeat myself?"

We all looked to the stern. Nuño wore a face of utter dismay.

"But, Captain…Now?"

All of us looked to the prow.

"It's as good a moment as any. Weigh anchor! To Trinidad!"

We all looked to the stern. Nuño remained still for a moment and then he stood up, his face set, and headed to the captain's quarters. Barracuda went ahead of him and entered first. We could all hear Nuño muttering before the door closed behind him: "My rotten foul luck!"

Nobody envied Nuño. We all knew that teaching Barracuda had to be worse than being nibbled to death by Two Molars. We also knew that, as if he didn't have enough to worry about, we would pester him with questions every time he emerged from the captain's quarters: "How's it going?" "What has he said about the letter H?" "Has he learned yet that 'all together' is written separate but the word 'separated' is written all together?"

Nuño didn't answer; he just cursed under his breath. For the next few days, as we sailed toward Trinidad, nobody could read a single line; Phineas' book was in Barracuda's chambers the entire time. The captain was stubborn about everything, and he thought that if he worked at it, he could learn to read in a day or two. You can imagine how upset he got when he discovered that this was impossible. After the end of the first lesson, we already heard him shout: "Ma-me-mi-mo-mu? What the barnacle is this ma-me-mi-mo-mu nonsense? Do you think I'm an idiot? I told you to teach me how to read, not to make me look like a fool!"

And this continued for the next three days. At one point, poor Nuño was trying to convince Barracuda that this was indeed the way one learns to read. Suddenly, we heard two curses in Turkish and the sound of something breaking. Then Nuño shot out of there like a bullet, tugging at the neck of his shirt and saying in a whisper, "It's impossible! I can't stand it anymore! Nobody could teach that animal how to read! Two Molars, I don't know why, but this is all your fault!"

On the fifth day, either because his patience had worn out or because he had run out of things to break, the captain left his quarters, stuck his hook into the helm, and remained on the bridge, glaring with undeserved hatred at poor Nuño, who seemed to grow older before our very eyes.

"He's in the denial phase..." Boasnovas said, looking at the captain.

"What?" asked Erik the Belgian.

"You know," Boasnovas responded. "That moment when reading is so difficult that you think you're a fool, and that everyone is laughing at you, and that you'll never be able to do it, and you blame everyone. It'll pass, you'll see."

"Shiver me timbers, you're a genius, Boasnovas!" Erik said with his hands on his hips. "It's incredible, but I know what you're talking about! We all do!"

And the rest of us agreed, looking at Barracuda. I don't know what he thought when he saw us all gawking and nodding at him because he turned his back on us and stared out to sea. Denial, plain as can be...

44

Trinidad is full of merchants, so you can find almost anything if you've got enough money. The city is full of people making deals of all sorts; on any corner you can see handshakes and people spitting onto the ground to seal the deal, not to mention one sort of fight or another.

It's not easy to buy and sell things between pirates and people of that ilk. Trust me on this one: a pirate would cut off his leg before he'd go back on his word. But let me also assure you that, in general, pirates don't place much value on their extremities; they know that appendages are easily lost in any skirmish.

With all this, I want to tell you that a pirate's word is worth what it's worth…and that depends directly on what he has to win or lose in the matter; therefore, be very careful.

This time, since the port of Trinidad isn't a safe place, Nuño remained on board the *Southern Cross* with half the crew, and the rest of us (and you know that included me) disembarked with the captain.

We walked through the streets as if we were a parade, all of us behind Barracuda, who went ahead with a firm step. Although it was a hot day, it was nice to stretch our legs. Suddenly, without saying a word, the captain stopped short; we all looked around for whatever had put him on alert. He turned his head slowly toward a doorway and then raised his head toward an enormous sign painted in blue above the door's lintel. His eyes grew big as saucers; he looked at all of us, and then without saying a word, he entered the house like a shot. Astonished, we remained on the threshold until we heard him ask from within, "Hey, young lady! Is this an inn?"

"Yes," came a female voice.

Barracuda emerged, looked up at the sign again and pointed at the blue letters while he moved his lips.

"It's an inn," he said at last, as if he had seen a ghost. "It wasn't here before, but now it's an inn," he read.

"Yes, Captain, that's what the sign says in big letters," Malik told him.

"Exactly," Barracuda answered in a whisper as if he were talking to himself. "That's what it says! Are you lot hungry? Let's have a drink!" he added, very excited, and went back inside.

"Now he's realized," the Whale said. I looked at him, and he tried to explain himself. "What this business of being able to read is like, I mean. It's like a deaf man hearing music for the first time…It must be like that."

We all went inside the inn. Barracuda was euphoric as if he had managed to swim around the Cape of Good Hope. He ordered beer for everyone and a root beer for me.

"So this is a new inn, eh?" a contented captain said, leaning on the bar. "Well! I had no idea! But, of course, I saw the sign above the door, and I said to myself, 'This is an inn, just like it says there in writing!'"

The innkeeper looked at us without the slightest degree of interest, to tell the truth. She couldn't have known that the captain was in a uniquely happy mood. Although we had won battles and

captured loot of gold and precious stones, that just-swallowed-vinegar look on his face never changed. The Barracuda's smile looked so strange to us because we had never seen it before.

And so, when we returned to the ship that night loaded with provisions, we were in such good humor as if we were returning from a party. As soon as we boarded, Nuño froze like a block of stone when Barracuda gave him a friendly hug and asked him how his day had been.

"My...My day? How was my day?" Nuño repeated, in shock. "I don't...I don't understand..."

"He found an inn all by himself," Boasnovas whispered to him; but, of course, with just that as a clue, Nuño didn't understand anything.

"My good Nuño!" the captain interrupted, giving him a friendly blow to the back. "It's not yet late, right? Come now, let's have a long reading lesson!" and he walked toward his quarters in a good mood. On reaching the door, he stopped short and read aloud: "'Cap-tain!' This is fantastic! They're everywhere! Letters, I mean! Who would have thought it!"

The next morning, Barracuda ordered us all on deck and to stand in silence. This happens only when it's a serious or

important situation. We were as quiet as pirates know how to be; but as soon as the captain began to speak, the deck was as silent as a grave.

"Crew! I will say this just once, and whoever doesn't follow my orders will wind up on the bottom of the sea! Nobody, I repeat *NOBODY,* once they step off this ship, will ever say that they know how to read, nor will anyone *ever* mention Phineas' book! We won't have a repeat of what happened on Española or Barbados: reading in front of just anyone, with the book visible to everyone. These are the secrets of the *Southern Cross.* I want to hear you each swear it!"

"But, Captain…," Boasnovas was the first to reply. "This is very difficult. How does one pretend not to know something… that you do know?"

"Easy, One-Eyed," Jack responded, "if they ask you, say you don't know it, and that's that."

"Sure, that's easy," Boasnovas answered. "But if they don't ask you? It's just, some things are obvious; you can't hide them away."

"But how are people going to know that you can read, you big mackerel?" Erik the Belgian told him, giving him a big slap on the back. "Do you think your face looks more clever now that you can read?"

"Of course, it's noticeable!" Boasnovas protested. "It's noticeable in everything! It's noticeable that you know things!"

"Wait," Jack said. "He's right. Let me give you an example. If you're being followed by some men who are trying to rob you, and you see a door that says 'Weapons' and another that says 'No exit,' you'll go through the first door without hesitating and never go through the second!"

"What kind of men are these who're following us?" John the Whale asked.

"What does that have to do with this?" Erik the Belgian complained, looking up into the sky for patience.

"It's to know if I can handle them," the Whale explained. "If it's just two or three…maybe I don't even need to run."

"This is not about that!" Boasnovas yelled at him, growing desperate. "You're right, it's noticeable! It's noticeable if you know how to read!"

"Or if they give you a bottle to drink, and it says 'Poison'?"

Malik entered the conversation. "Do you need to drink it so they don't suspect? I don't think I could!"

"Or if they want to sell you a barrel of rum," Two Molars interjected, "and you see that the barrel says 'Beans'! I'm not paying for beans at the price of rum!"

"You'd be a fool if you did!" One-Legged Jack said, patting Two Molars' arm in support. "Now, if I get ahold of the guy who did my tattoo, I'll make him drink all of those inks of his!"

"Everybody, calm down now," Nuño said at last, always the voice of reason. "If the guys who are chasing you don't know how to read, how will they know that you've chosen the door to the arms room instead of the one with no exit?"

"That's true!" I nodded. "Nobody would notice! At most, if you choose the right door, and if you don't drink the poison, and if you discover that the shopkeeper tried to swindle you with a barrel of beans, they'll just think you're the luckiest pirate in the world!"

The pirates laughed heartily. Except Barracuda, of course, who, without a doubt, was pleased, but let's not exaggerate. Instead, he suddenly shouted, "Enough! Stop with all this stupidity!"

Everyone shut up. When there was silence, the captain continued, serious as a heart attack:

"Can't you all see? All the pirates of these oceans know that I've been searching for Krane's treasure for years. In Maracaibo rumors were already circulating that I had found it, don't you remember? And now, suddenly, it turns out that this entire crew of blockheads suddenly knows how to read! What do you want them to think? That we've swallowed a scribe? Why does a bunch of wretches like us even *need* to read? And what will happen when we find the many riches that Phineas' book could bring us? In case any of you hasn't realized, you're not exactly discreet when you've got money, you blarney fools! Don't you think that someone could draw the connection between this sudden interest in reading with, look at that, what a coincidence, this band of idiots suddenly always has their pockets full of coins?"

"Hey, One-Legged Jack," Boasnovas whispered. "Is it just me, or is the captain insulting us, gratuitous like?"

"No, it's not just you," Jack answered. "Blockheads, wretches, fools, idiots…He's not pulling punches…"

"I won't run unnecessary risks!" Barracuda continued. "Many would kill to have Phineas' book…if they even suspected that it existed! And our enemies have too much free time to think; perhaps one of them will come to the conclusion that old Krane left something that can be read…You know what I say is true! So you'll keep pointing with a finger at what you want to order in taverns, and you'll ask where the public bathrooms are although you can see the sign right before your noses!"

"It will be our secret, then," John the Whale declared solemnly, making an X with his finger across his chest and then spitting on the deck. "A pirate secret of the most important kind!"

The rest of us imitated him. This was an oath of utmost significance. Any pirate would snitch on you if you broke the oath, and the rest would treat you like a pariah. This was a serious promise. Nobody forced you to swear a pirate oath, but if you swore it, you'd better not treat it like it was a joke….

We could say, then, that the *Southern Cross* was the ship with the most strangely mysterious crew that ever sailed the Caribbean sea. We had a treasure, but only we knew that it was a treasure; we knew how to read, but we had to pretend to be a group of ignorant clodhoppers. Who would have imagined all of this, even just one month earlier?

Although it might seem strange, all of this brought us closer together. We were like members of a secret clan, full of winks, elbowings, and laughing at in-jokes. We got a kick out of asking for the bakery right in front of the sign, or asking the waiter for chicken after having seen on the menu, written in enormous letters, that they served ONLY fish. It cracked us up, although we were the only ones who understood why.

And, of course, we continued reading whenever we had a free moment from the obligations of sailing. Our lessons continued. And now it wasn't just Two Molars who acted as our teacher, but all of us, with greater patience or not, helping the slower readers among us. You can't believe how difficult it is to teach something that you know and see so clearly when you can't manage to get the other person to understand it! Without a doubt, Two Molars deserved a statue in his honor in some idyllic place!

We spent two weeks in Trinidad; it took Nuño that long to get a good price for the fabrics we hadn't sold to Bruno, the fabric merchant. On Thursday of the second week (I remember it well) something happened that you should know about—something that showed us definitively that Phineas Krane's book not only said things that were true but that it was a real treasure bound in leather.

I think that none of us ever thought much again of the incident in Barbados with Bruno, and by the time Nuño finally sold the kerchiefs and brocades, we had even forgotten all about it. But if I haven't already said this, I'll say it now: it's very dangerous to offend a guy like that because they live for their image. They can't appear to be soft or let people think that someone's done them wrong and gotten away with it. And since vengeance is a dish best served cold, Bruno Castilfierro prepared a trap for us in Trinidad to retaliate for Barracuda not signing his contract and refusing to sell him the merchandise. I told you we would hear from him again.

It was night, a night as black as the eyes of a cockroach. Only fifteen of us disembarked, including Barracuda; the rest stayed on the *Southern Cross*. We headed to the Tavern of the Port for dinner. It was very late, and in one of the alleys that opens onto the pier, suddenly, our way was blocked by ten or twelve men with covered faces. From behind us, at the other end of the alley, another twenty men, at least, all armed to the teeth, closed off any hope of retreat. Pay attention; things are about to get serious…

Barracuda moved ahead of us and unsheathed his saber so quickly that even we were surprised. And, of course, so were all of the men who stood before him. As usual, I was squeezed

between John the Whale and Erik the Belgian, who brandished his ax with the dexterity of two men. I was surrounded, therefore, by a protective wall of pirates.

"Which of you is Barracuda?" called out a masked man—a broad-shouldered, muscled sort with a strange English accent.

"Who wants to know?" the captain replied, taking a step forward. "My mother always told me never to talk to strangers…."

"Well, what do you know? We've got ourselves a comedian!" the masked man responded and lowered the kerchief that covered his mouth and nose. "I'm Orson the Scotsman. You've offended a good friend of mine, and I'm going to teach you a lesson like nothing you've ever seen before!"

It was evident from far away that these men didn't know Barracuda. Nobody who knew him, even a little bit, would have ever dared to speak to him like that. He merely smiled, as he did when he was truly angry, with that smile that was scarier than Davy Jones's locker.

"Well," he said slowly. "So a friend sent you…And does that

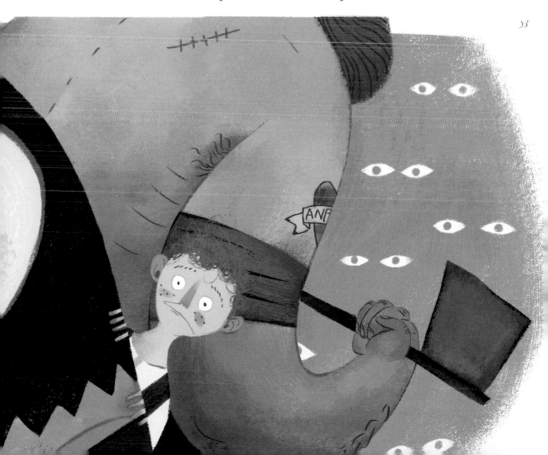

friend have a name? I'm a pirate. I've managed to upset a lot of people, given that I make my living by attacking ships and plundering them for loot. But, why hasn't this friend come in person? This friend wouldn't happen to be some little old lady, who had to send a bunch of blockheads to do her dirty work for them..."

We could all see that the big guy didn't like the sound of this, nor did his companions.

"Orson the Scotsman...Orson the Scotsman...Where have I heard that name before...?" Erik the Belgian muttered in front of me, although nobody paid any attention to him.

The situation was tricky. They had twice our numbers, and they also carried firearms as well as swords. But, one thing is certain, you could say anything you wanted about the crew of the *Southern Cross*...except that we were cowards! The Whale threw the first punch to a man as large and fat as he, who'd been glaring at him with clenched teeth. After that, sandwiched as I was between enormous John and Erik, I can't tell you with much precision what happened, but I could hear blows falling left and right. I saw at least seven of our opponents flying through the air, and quite a few teeth were spat out (some even by our side). We defended ourselves fiercely; even I added a bite or two to the fight, on those who fell between the Whale's feet. But in the middle of the fight (when our forces were most evenly balanced), one of our opponents pulled out the arquebus that was strapped to his back and shot One-Legged Jack. We all froze in horror, knowing that he would fall and strike the ground. But no one was more surprised than Jack when he didn't fall, at least not right away; he touched his chest, searching for the wound, when suddenly he fell on his side with a loud crunching of splinters. He'd been shot in his false leg!

"Scurvy squidface!" Jack shouted. "They've ruined my leg! And it cost me three doubloons!"

After a tense silence, more firearms appeared: various mausers, arquebuses, and even some short pistols. None of them, unfortunately, were ours. Since we were on our way to dinner, we had only our swords and daggers with us. And in my case, I had only a slingshot. What did you expect? I was only eleven!

"Splendid; you've killed a wooden leg," the captain said. "Are you happy or will we have to seriously hurt you, Scotsman?"

"Bruno won't settle for so little, Barracuda. He won't stand for being disrespected," Orson replied, pointing his arquebus at the captain.

"So you're here on behalf of that swindling cur Castilfierro! I should have known! That stinking rat coward has to send others to take care of business for him!"

Suddenly, Erik reached up and grabbed his own head, trying to find within his brains something he couldn't manage to grab ahold of. Suddenly, he pushed us back with one of his big, meaty hands and stepped between Barracuda and the Scotsman.

"Orson the Scotsman! Orson MacGowan, from Aberdeen! It is you! I knew I recognized you! Tall, strong, and with a scar on your eyebrow from when you fell off a half-tamed horse when you were a child!"

The Scotsman froze in place on hearing his full name and the city of his birth. Then he touched his right eyebrow where, effectively, he had the mark of that ancient wound. None of us could see it well in the moonlight, but the expression on Orson's face clearly showed us that it was there.

"Where do you know me from, Frenchman? I don't think I've ever seen you in my life…"

"I'm Belgian," Erik said loudly. "And it's true, you don't know me. But I know you, by your reputation. Orson MacGowan! No one in Scotland doesn't know that name! I was there a long time ago, back when I was young, and you were already a legend. Your exploits on the battlefield are famous!" He turned toward us. "Did you know that MacGowan means 'son of Gowan'? What a great man, your father! I didn't find anyone there who had a bad opinion of him! And how he rode a horse!"

We were all dumbfounded. When had Erik the Belgian ever been in Scotland? We all thought that he had come to the Caribbean when he was a lad, as a stowaway on a German merchant ship. But what was even stranger to us was that, to our astonishment, as Orson stood before us, his eyes filled up with tears!

"You…you knew me pa?" the Scotsman stuttered, lowering his weapon.

"Of course! I'll never forget him. A tall man with white hair, who lived in an enormous estate called Shetland, on the outskirts of Aberdeen. There he welcomed me and my brother Frans when, one stormy night, we lost our way near there. He gave us dinner and served us one of his most cherished wines; you know, from the bodega he has below the chapel…A great man, he seemed to us! Who could've told me that years later, on the other side of the world, I'd meet his son! You should have heard the pride and affection with which he spoke about you, lad!"

The poor Orson couldn't hold back any longer and started bawling like a baby, embracing Erik. We couldn't believe what we were seeing, but the men who were with the Scotsman were really discombobulated; they didn't know what to do! It was the Scotsman himself who put an end to that strange situation.

"Lower your weapons!" he shouted at his companions, releasing the Belgian. "Any man my father has welcomed into his home is a friend of mine! It's been many moons since I left my beloved Scotland…Please, come and have a drink with us! Barracuda, accept my apologies. It was just a commission, nothing personal…But now, after speaking to me of my Pa…" his eyes grew misty again, and he put an arm around Erik's shoulders.

"Well," the Whale said, "the fact is that we haven't eaten yet."

And so everyone went to the tavern together. That's how things are between pirates; you never know what might happen. It was a fun night, to tell the truth. Those men told some fantastic stories. I learned something important that night: if you have the chance, and you talk with people instead of fighting, you'll surely discover you have more to win that way.

That evening, I kept thinking about the jokes and the laughter we would have lost if things had finished off in that alleyway in blows, instead of here in the tavern, between chicken wings and baked sea bass. The Belgian and the Scotsman seemed like childhood pals: they laughed like little kids and hugged one another like old comrades. Barracuda was mistrustful at first, but as the night advanced he managed to relax, and while he didn't say much, he ate plenty. I even think I saw him try to smile, really smile, a few times.

The other pirates accompanied us back to the ship and bid us farewell like soul brothers, with shoving and slaps on the neck; you know, like pirates. By the time we climbed the gangplanks, those who had remained aboard were already asleep.

"Oh my, Erik, what luck," Two Molars said in the darkness on deck.

"Well, yes…," the Belgian replied.

"Yes! Especially me," protested One-Legged Jack, who was half-carried by Boasnovas. "I've lost my leg…again!"

"I mean about Scotland," Two Molars explained. "How lucky that you had been in his home, there in Scotland, and that you met his father!"

"I've never been in Scotland in my life," Erik replied calmly.

"You've never…" I spluttered, having swallowed the entire story.

"Are you kidding?" he answered. "Never!"

"Explain yourself, Belgian!" Barracuda intervened. "How could you know so many details about his father, his house…?"

Erik the Belgian slowly looked at us one after another, then he smiled from ear to ear and finally said, "It wasn't me who knew him nor who had been in his house and dined with his father. It was Phineas! Phineas did that! I couldn't remember where I had heard the name Orson the Scotsman before. Until I realized that I hadn't heard it. I had read it! Chapter Ten of the

book! Everything I said is in there. I think I even used the very same words that old Krane wrote!"

We were silent for a full minute at least, long enough to think back over what had happened during that strange night. Then, suddenly, we started laughing with such gusto that they must have heard us far across the city. Many of those who had remained on board woke up; among them Nuño, who always slept like a log.

We spent all night retelling our story to the rest of the crew who hadn't gone ashore. We also read Chapter Ten of Phineas' book and laughed wholeheartedly as we walked around the deck. Barracuda watched us from the bridge, lest a smile escape him, leading us to think he might have a sense of humor.

The stories in Phineas' book were proving to be entirely true as we could see for ourselves. So Barracuda, who was nobody's fool, decided to take a step ahead of events. Instead of letting chance lead us toward something that appeared in the book, he decided to take the initiative and hunt down the things Krane described. We had a stack of trustworthy information to take advantage of, and if we played our cards right, we could gain riches by the bucketful.

The following days, still in the Port of Trinidad, the book never left the captain's quarters. Nuño and he seemed to be looking for something. And on the morning of the second day, they must have found it because we could hear Nuño shouting, "Here it is! I knew it! If the book says so, then it must be true! It does exist!" Right after, they emerged onto the deck, and we were all summoned once again. Nuño was carrying Phineas' book and wearing a smug look on his face.

"I told you! At last, our luck will change," Barracuda began, with something that only those of us who knew him well could recognize as cheerfulness. "Skeptics said that Krane's book was just a bedtime story, something to read on long winter nights, by the light of a fire, but I always knew that it was true."

"But, Captain, what are you talking about?" Two Molars interrupted.

"I'm talking about a loot of precious stones that many believe is a legend. But we are going to find it because now we know *where* to look…!"

"But, what is it?" I asked, unable to bear all this intrigue.

"The coffer of Fung Tao!" Barracuda exclaimed in a voice like a thunderbolt.

The dead silence that followed was like the calm on the sea

just before a colossal storm. It was as if the entire world was paralyzed. The men looked at one another, their eyes betraying fear, suspicion, incredulity—all mixed together.

"What is the coffer of Fung Tao?" I asked Boasnovas, who, at my side, opened his only eye so wide it looked as if he were trying to compensate for the one he lacked. "I've never heard of it..."

"It's not good to speak of this Chinese pirate," he answered in a very soft voice. "Nor to say his name on a ship; it brings bad luck..."

"Those are old wive's tales!" Erik the Belgian interjected. "Stories to frighten newbies and kids on stormy days! A Chinese pirate? Who has ever seen that?"

"They're not old wive's tales," Russian Kitty said from behind us. "And don't speak his name again!"

Even the captain was surprised by this turn of events.

You will say, and with reason, that you haven't heard of Russian Kitty until now. That's true. I can't go into every detail about every single pirate on the *Southern Cross* and what each did every time something happened; if I did, we'd never finish. I am telling you, above all, about the ones I interacted with the most. The Russian, in fact, spoke so seldom that some of us (myself included) didn't even know what his voice sounded like. He learned to read along with the rest of us, but silently because we never heard him repeat aloud a single word. He only stared a lot, like an owl, and nodded his head up and down or left to right. The Kitty was a pale man, short and thin; he took care of the weapons and cannons along with Boasnovas. You wouldn't believe how strong he was, given how scrawny he looked. He had been part of the crew of the *Southern Cross* for almost ten years, and, in truth, the only things we knew about him were that his name was Leon Paulovich and that he came from Siberia, deep in Russia. But, as you've already seen, pirates love to joke; since little Leon was not big like a lion, they began to call him the Russian Kitty. That's how I was introduced to him.

"I've also heard the story about this Chinese pirate..." the Whale said. "But they told me it was a hoax that ran through the taverns, a bunch of lies to make greedy pirates go mad."

"It's not a hoax," Barracuda said, "nor a legend. It's completely true. It's in the book."

"Come on! Nobody is going to believe that!" Erik the

Belgian protested, looking at the rest of us. "Many brave men have lost their senses searching for this treasure. Even the Pirate Morgan himself went in search of it! He lifted every rock on Martinique looking for it and lost almost his entire crew! And he didn't find it!"

"He didn't find it because the coffer *was never on Martinique*!" Nuño explained, holding up the book. "It's all in here: the story of Fung Tao and, what's more important, the exact place where Phineas, with his own hands, hid the coffer...Until now, everything that old Krane has written has been true. Why would he lie about this?"

"You've said the Chinese pirate's name three times now," the Kitty said. "This is not good...Not good..."

Heavens above! Five sentences in one day! Without a doubt, something was going to happen!

My *Life as a Pirate* by Phineas Johnson Krane. Chapter Fifteen.
I will copy it here just as it appears in the book:

Southern Sea of China. It wasn't the first
time that we had heard talk of Fung Tao. Our
paths had never crossed, despite his being
a pirate famous throughout the Southern
Seas. Between the Sea of Java and the Gulf
of Siam, nothing moved without his knowing
about it. The ships that traded silk and the
merchants of the English Armada feared him,
fleeing as soon as they saw on the horizon the
red sails of his *Dragon's Blood*, an imposing
ship made from light bamboo that flew over
the waves. His flag inspired the same dread:
a red dragon with a skull between its claws
upon a black background. He was almost
untouchable because the emperor of China
protected him and had even freed him on a
few occasions from the jails of Sumatra and
Malaysia, absolute cesspools where harder
men have rotted for years.

I had already decided to return to the
Caribbean, when—because it was my fate
or his disgrace—we met by chance during
a game of cards on the island of Formosa,
off the coast of China. He seemed to me too
young for the fame that preceded him: he was
barely twenty-five. He dressed like most men
from that area: in a tunic with pants beneath
it, white with gold trim; and he wore his hair
in a long braid, with a little hat or skull cap
of the same fabric as his outfit. Everything

screamed wealth. But he was not alone. Two evil-looking henchmen from his crew stood behind him. They were tiny and thin but rumored to be so skilled in fighting with their hands and feet that they could each fight off eight men at once.

That blasted Fung Tao played well and bet a lot. From a red leather sack, he carelessly pulled gold coins as if they held no value. I don't trust people who don't respect money...I don't remember if I won or lost in that round of cards because I was distracted with watching Fung Tao's every move. He didn't say much during our card game, but as soon as dinner and wine had their effect, the other participants loosened their tongues. Those fools joked about a red coffer decorated with two black dragons, where apparently Fung Tao guarded his most prized pieces: diamonds, pearls, rubies. I also knew that he was so mistrusting that he always carried it with him. On board his ship, instead of caching it with his other treasures, he slept with his head resting upon the coffer. All this I discovered without asking a single wretched question. I would have hung them all for lesser indiscretions.

We finished in the wee hours of the morning, and when I returned to the *Prince of Antigua*, I already knew I wanted that little pillow full of riches for myself. The occasion was favorable: I would carry out a masterstroke of a raid and then disappear forever from those latitudes. I was born to battle with soldiers, not with merchants. And if I remained in the Southern Seas for much longer, I would wind up turning into a cursed spice merchant myself...

To be victorious, I had to overcome these obstacles: Fung Tao's crew (no less than thirty men who were all expert fighters); and his ship, which was lighter and faster than my own, and with which he could surely overtake us. Helped by Khaled, my second in command, I prepared a precise plan by which, using only six men and in less than an hour, we would make off with the loot. Khaled the Syrian was as tiny as a child but as clever as the devil himself.

The *Dragon's Blood* was anchored in a very broad cover, almost half a mile from the port of Formosa. I sent as my spy Layo the Sevillian, a Spaniard capable of hiding even in a flat, open desert. He spent two days on the coast, in the sun, so motionless that no one noticed him sitting among the rocks of the cliffs. That's how good he was at what he did. When the sun set on the second day, he returned to our ship with a detailed account of the guard shifts, the crew's habits, and their weapons, and he drew us a detailed plan of Fung Tao's ship.

With the plan perfectly drawn up, I let Layo rest. I formed a small group of five of my best men: Khaled the Syrian, Hans the Beast, Silent George, Congo, Pancoli the Sicilian, and also myself.

First, we sailed the *Prince of Antigua* onto the open sea, on the other side of the estuary of the port, to ensure a quick escape. We dropped anchor, and I ordered the entire crew to be on high-alert to set sail as soon as our group of six returned to the ship with the coffer.

There was a new moon, and the night was eerily dark. We approached the *Dragon's Blood* in a little boat, carrying only our weapons and flints to set fires. We paddled to the ship as silently as possible. We managed to arrive undetected, accomplishing half of our surprise mission. George lit some kindling and placed two points of fire on the hull of the *Dragon's Blood*: one fire where Layo said the hold was located, with all the provisions; and the other fire (with a longer wick) under the gunpowder storage.

At the ship's stern, I went up first, and the rest followed me. Just as Hans stepped onto the deck of the *Dragon's Blood*, we smelled burning rice. The pantry, in the prow, was already burning fiercely. The ship's crew began shouting. Right before us, under the command bridge, Fung Tao emerged from his quarters, in his underclothes and with his hair a tangled mess. The night was so black that, amid the anxious shouting, Congo and I managed to slip into Fung Tao's chambers while my other men kept watch. And there... on Fung Tao's bed...by all the sea's dead, was the black and red coffer!

We grabbed it immediately, but as we bolted back out, our luck ended. We ran straight into three Chinese crewmen who began shouting as if they'd seen the devil himself. Without hesitating, Congo tossed the chest into our small boat; then he threw me overboard and jumped after me. Above us, still on the ship, my other men fought tooth and nail against Fung Tao's crew. Suddenly, Hans jumped, followed by

Silent George and the Sicilian. Right then, an enormous explosion ripped through the gunpowder chamber. Half the ship blew apart with pieces flying through the air amid the crash of breaking bamboo, and Khaled splashed near us like a sack of potatoes. We heaved him onto the boat, while all around us, it was raining Chinese crewmen into the sea. Some tried to climb into our boat, but the Sicilian fended them off while Congo, Hans, and George rowed with all their might toward our ship.

As we rowed away, the *Dragon's Blood* was fully engulfed in flames. Total confusion reigned; flames illuminated the sky, and shouting and cursing filled the night.

We paddled furiously and finally reached the *Prince of Antigua*; it was ready to set sail. We climbed aboard, pulling the anchor with us to save time. We knew Fung Tao was smart enough and influential enough that we couldn't underestimate his ability to react, so we had to escape from Formosa immediately, abandoning the Southern Seas as quickly as possible. Not only had we earned the enmity of the terrible Fung Tao, but also that of his friend, the emperor of China. May the devil's lair swallow us! We must never return!

For months, now in Caribbean waters, I carried the coffer with me. But it was only a matter of time before some other nasty adventurer like myself would learn of its existence and try to steal the coffer from me—history repeating itself. I decided to hide it until things cooled off. What's more, stories ran rampant of a mysterious ship, full of Chinese men who searched unceasingly throughout the Caribbean for a pirate who sounded suspiciously like me. I never saw Fung Tao, that's true, but many nights I felt his gaze on the back of my neck, searching restlessly for his dragon coffer.

Yes, it was necessary for our treasure to sleep until the whole business was forgotten. Khaled said he knew the perfect hiding spot. It was in a place so dangerous that only someone sick with madness would attempt to enter it. It had an entrance so hidden that no one would ever find it. And its passageway was so narrow that only someone small and thin would be able to squeeze through all the way to the end, where the coffer would be placed. It seemed perfect, and Khaled was trustworthy.

Following Khaled's indications, we set sail for the island of Dominica, where we docked the *Prince of Antigua*. Then, Khaled and I prepared a small launch, and in the middle of the night, we slipped away with the coffer. At dawn, we were on the high sea. With tremendous effort, we reached Guadeloupe, to the north, our true destination. Guadeloupe is actually two islands separated by a narrow arm of the sea. We headed to the largest of the two, to the west, called Basse-Terre, a wild, green island full of waterfalls and trees. To the south of the island, is an enormous volcano called Soufrière, which means "sulfur" in French. It was as if we were at the door of the devil's furnace; the ground smolders and the air burns. That's how terrible this place is, and that's where the Syrian led me.

I drew the route so as not to forget it. And by the devil's whiskers, it's a good thing I did so, because two years later, my faithful Khaled died of a fever from an illness he caught in Barbados. This is the map.

Old Phineas did me a favor: if he hadn't included the warning from Khaled about "only someone small and thin could fit," I would have been left behind on the ship. It was a dangerous excursion, and the other pirates didn't want to take me along. But I was the smallest person on the crew. Well, the truth is, I wasn't that much smaller than Russian Kitty, but he wouldn't let go of the mast, even when threatened with a dunking into boiling water. Such was his terror about everything that had to do with Tung Tao and his coffer.

The *Southern Cross* dropped anchor in an uninhabited area to quell the suspicions of the French detachment billeted on the island. We were six who disembarked—Barracuda, Nuño, the Whale, One-Eyed Boasnovas, Erik the Belgian, and I—like the six who had stolen the chest from the *Dragon's Blood*. I don't know if the captain did this on purpose, but I like these kinds of coincidences.

We crossed a thick and humid jungle. We were eaten alive by enormous mosquitoes that made a deafening buzz when they flew. That's how our misfortunes began when a mosquito bit Boasnovas on the eyelid of his only eye, and the bite swelled up into such a large welt that he was now truly blind. We couldn't send him back because he couldn't see his hand in front of his face, so the captain ordered me to take care of him and to guide him through the underbrush. Poor Boasnovas fell often, banging his head against branches and constantly sticking his feet into stinking puddles. At first, it made me laugh, but soon it wasn't funny because with him walking behind me and holding onto my shoulder, when he stumbled, we both stumbled. But I couldn't get mad; I would look at him and see that single eye, which had swelled bigger and bigger until it looked like a peach, and I just couldn't stop laughing.

Soon, our path ascended steeply. The landscape was now barren; it was as if the vegetation had suddenly disappeared. In front of us rose a bare mountain, without a peak, as if it had been sliced off. It was the Soufrière volcano. We were still near the foot of the volcano and already the heat was unbearable. We climbed along a narrow, steep path. The rocky terrain was so sheer; it was as if it had been cut by a knife. At times, we had to

advance almost on our hands and knees, with Boasnovas banging his head into my backside every time we stopped.

Nuño had copied the map from Phineas' book, and it turned out to be quite precise.

"Well…" Nuño said, examining the map. "Now the difficult part begins. We need to go up along there."

He pointed to something that no one in their right mind would call a path: an inclined track, suitable for mountain goats only. The end—somewhere up the volcano—was obscured by a fog of sulfur and smoke.

"*Now* the difficult part begins…?" complained Boasnovas, who of course couldn't see what we saw. "You've got to be kidding me! My elbows and knees are scraped raw from banging into things! And now it's going to get worse?"

"From here on, we advance single file," Barracuda ordered. "I will go first. Whale, you'll go last, right behind Sparks and Boasnovas. Be careful; this trail is extremely narrow, and you can hardly see a thing."

We began to climb with great effort. I suppose I wasn't the only one who wondered how we would get down again if, as Phineas promised, up above us, in some cranny of this terrible place, was Fung Tao's coffer. Nonetheless—and this is another

lesson that I learned in those years as a pirate—one must worry about things when the moment comes, not before and not after.

With every step we took, the air became more unbreathable and the path even steeper. Behind me, Boasnovas was constantly slipping, yanking on the rope that connected him to me and kicking his feet in the Whale's face. He even pulled off my boot a few times. At last, the Whale couldn't stand it anymore and suddenly shouted into the silence of the volcano, "Captain! Permission to change the order!"

"As you wish, Whale, but don't shout," Barracuda answered him.

Then, enormous Whale grabbed Boasnovas as if he were a bundle and threw him over his shoulder. Boasnovas protested for a while, but everyone ignored him. We advanced more quickly this way, and the Whale lugged Boasnovas as if he weighed nothing.

We reached an area, on the edge of a precipice, where the path was barely as wide as two hands placed side by side. The fog prevented us from seeing to the bottom, but I assure you, had you been there, you wouldn't have wanted to test for yourselves where it was. We continued our ascent, scooting sideways, our backs pressed against the rocky wall.

"If you don't stop squirming, Boasnovas, I'm going to tie your head to my belt and leave you dangling like a keychain," Whale said, utterly serious, and Boasnovas stopped flailing his arms and protesting.

The Whale looked like he was wearing a scarf—a scarf that had a patch over a missing eye and the other eye swollen to the size of a small melon (it hadn't stopped swelling).

"Here it is," Nuño said suddenly, and we immediately stopped.

"Here?" Erik asked, looking all around. "Here where?"

"There," Nuño said, pointing ahead a few steps. To the right, a short distance away, was a hole in the ground, out of which spewed steam and a reddish glow.

"That's the entrance?" the Whale asked. "It looks like an oven! I don't think I can go down there."

"You're going to have to!" Barracuda replied, approaching the hole. "Are you certain this is the place the book describes, Nuño?"

"Not the least doubt, Captain. The description is clear."

"All right then," exclaimed the brave Barracuda, and he jumped inside the hole without hesitating.

That's how he was: the bravest there ever was. Of course, after that, who could balk at going down? Erik held his enormous ax in his teeth and jumped after him. Without warning, the Whale tossed Boasnovas into the hole. Then the Whale went down, but not without effort. For a moment, Nuño and I thought that the Whale was stuck, blocking our way down and trapping the others below. Finally, we helped push the Whale—as he huffed and puffed and sucked in his belly as much as he could—through the hole. It was like trying to squeeze squishy bread dough into a small tube.

Then, hands appeared from the hole, and I heard the Belgian tell me, "Come on, Sparks! I'll help you!"

You've come so far on this journey with me; now is not the time to back out. Although I assure you, if you had really been there, even the hair on the back of your neck would have stood on end. But this was no time for cowardice! Shout as I did: "For Barracuda, after the coffer!" And leap down into the hole with me!

I stuck my feet into the crevice, and Erik from below and Nuño up top helped me into the hole. It was as if the earth itself were swallowing me; that's how I felt.

If that crack wasn't the very belly of a furious beast, I wouldn't know any other way to describe it. The stone walls were red as blood, steam and hot water spewed forth from every fissure in the rock, and the air was suffocating.

"It's this way," said Nuño, who'd followed me down.

The cavern went even deeper into the mountain, toward the very entrails of the volcano. To not repeat myself, I won't recount every time Boasnovas banged against everything that jutted into the passageway. I'll only say that he once bumped his head against the floor, but without even falling first. Don't ask me how he did it; I didn't understand it either. At one point, the passageway became so narrow that the Whale's entire body was completely sandwiched between the rocky walls.

"Aha!" Barracuda exclaimed up ahead. "Yellow! On the map, the passage is marked in yellow."

We moved closer. In the upper part of the wall, we could see a small hole that looked like it was painted yellow on the inside.

"It looks very deep," Nuño said, peering inside. "And it's narrow…Sparks! Here's where your job begins. Climb in there and pull the coffer out. It's in there."

I felt really important at that moment. The opening was so tiny that only I could fit in. And then I became a little afraid, let's be honest…Being afraid (let me tell you, since I've felt the entire spectrum of fear) isn't a bad thing; everyone feels it, even the biggest pirates, although they deny it. What is truly important is to face your fears and not let them control you.

"Captain, I think it would be a good idea to tie a cord around the boy's foot, in case he gets stuck or can't handle the weight of the coffer," Erik proposed.

"What's going on?" Boasnovas asked. "Are we there yet? It's so terribly warm here!" He was bewildered by his blindness and all the blows to his head from walking into things.

"Come on, boy!" Whale encouraged me. "I'll hold the cord, and I'll pull you out of there if you find yourself in trouble. I promise you."

I didn't doubt that he would. Although he never said so, I knew that the Whale was very fond of me and that if something were to happen to me in there, he'd break down the wall with his teeth to get me out.

So, summarizing the situation, I was about to enter the place where supposedly old Krane had hidden a coffer full of riches—the coffer that he, in the distant Southern Seas, had robbed from the *Dragon's Blood*. The pirates tied a cord around my ankle, and away I went, into a dark and narrow hole in search of a legendary pirate treasure. That was my life then! And I can't say it was a bad life, not in the least!

The place was truly narrow, it smelled like rotting eggs, and I couldn't see a thing. I inched along on my belly, moving forward by thrusting my hands in front of me and feeling my way. Everything was hot and damp at the same time. The voices of the others grew farther and farther away, and I began to think that the book had tricked us but good when, suddenly, my hands touched something in front of me—something smooth, with edges, and corners. Oh my! Could it be the coffer? It must be because what were the chances that some other person had hidden, precisely here, a different box, coffer, or whatever it was? I felt around until I found what seemed to be a side handle, and I tugged it with all my might. Then I shouted for the pirates to pull me out (and with me, the coffer), and that's what they did.

As they hauled me out of that dark tunnel, the light that came in from the mouth of the hole, behind me, gradually let me see what I was pulling by the handle. First I could make out the red color of the box and then…there they were, even if worn and dusty: two dragons, facing one another!

And so it was: I was the first to see it once again, many years after Phineas and Khaled the Syrian had seen it for the last time: the red and black coffer of Fung Tao.

Imagine this: ten years' of birthday parties, a lifetime of Christmases and Mardis Gras, two weddings, and five years' of Sundays. Now take all those celebrations, mix them up, and multiply them by twelve. The result would not even come close to the blow-out party that the pirates threw when we (and the coffer) returned to the *Southern Cross*.

As is customary on pirate crews, the booty was split between everyone. Barracuda summoned us to the deck, and Nuño gave each of us a portion, depending on the value of each piece: two rubies and a diamond; or five aquamarines and two emeralds; and pearls, sapphires, amber, and jade.

I desperately wanted to keep, as a memento of that adventure, a valuable medallion that showed Fung Tao's two facing dragons, carved in black jet and mounted in gold and decorated with ivory. Since I was the one who pulled the coffer from the hole, nobody refused. Little did I know then the problems this would cause! But let's not get ahead of ourselves, I still have much more to tell you.

Here's another pirate fact you should know: pirates don't manage to keep their riches for very long. Another lesson I learned from these men is that what comes easily, goes easily. They can go for ages without a single escudo and then, suddenly, have enough gold doubloons to fill a beer pitcher. When that happens, nobody is more generous than a pirate. They'll treat you to food and drink until you fall on the floor, just because you're passing by the door of the tavern where they are or because you greet them by the lifting of your eyebrows (if you have them).

Unfortunately, I can't fully describe for you what happened over the next four days because, by the second day, I was exhausted and fell asleep in the corner. But what I did witness was unforgettable: scruffy pirates, their faces burned by gunpowder and the sun, wearing tattered clothes adorned with hundreds of jewels. Colorful, sparkly gems hung from their ears, their foreheads, their handkerchiefs, and their hats. The ship shone brightly as if hundreds of colorful lanterns were scattered around the deck.

Boasnovas, who now began to see through his swollen eye, played the accordion (oh, did I not mention this talent of his?) with such zest that he wound up breaking the bellows. But nobody noticed until a day and a half later, such was the noise those fellows made with their singing.

Two Molars started to dance, and there was no way to stop him. He went round and round the deck like a spinning top. I had never seen him like this, and I fell to the floor laughing. But he didn't care; he lifted up the legs of his pants as if they were a skirt and took little steps forward and back like a damsel. With a brilliant smile, Malik, to partner Two Molars in the dance, made some impressive leaps, higher than a meter and a half. The Whale, for his part, danced by moving—not his entire enormous body—just his two index fingers from side to side, while he closed his eyes and made little faces. One-Legged Jack, who still hadn't had a chance to buy himself a new leg, propped himself up as best he could with a leg from an old chair. Since the chair leg was much longer than his real leg, he went up and down by more than a head with every step he took. And I broke my one pair of boots by leaping about the ship like a madman. I laughed so hard that my jaw hurt for at least a week after.

The captain watched us from a certain distance. Don't for a moment think that Barracuda was going to dance or sing. You don't know him if you could imagine that! But I knew (because I'm clever) that he was enormously pleased. At last, he could give his men a treasure, just as he had promised them.

It was the longest, craziest, most fun party of my entire life, and that's saying a lot because, I assure you, I've been to plenty. When it was over, the *Southern Cross* was like a ghost ship, plagued with pirates sleeping everywhere, their feet swollen inside their boots from hours of dancing, and their throats hoarse from shouting and singing. We slept completely through the fifth day. The entire ship was an enormous snore that I'm sure could be heard even in Barbados.

On the morning of the sixth day, Barracuda got fed up with seeing us sleep like big lumps. He bellowed for us to swab the deck. He commanded that we use so much water, it was as if he were going to wash us all away and dump us into the sea. If we had fought tooth and nail against the English Armada in a narrow alleyway, we couldn't have been more exhausted. I was sticky with sweat, and through the holes in my ruined boots, I could see that my feet were black with filth. My feet hurt so much that I almost envied One-Legged Jack, who, with just one foot, must have hurt only half as much as I did.

We moved the ship from where we'd anchored and headed to the port of Basse-Terre, the capital of Guadeloupe. It was a clean and pretty city, occupied now by the French. We docked the *Southern Cross*. We had the advantage of nobody knowing that such a magnificent treasure had been sleeping for ages, right under their noses; therefore, no one would ever suspect that we had found such a treasure and that it was on board our ship right now. It was a perfect situation. We disembarked calmly, like fifty-three honorable travelers who had reached Guadeloupe in search of peace and quiet.

We dispersed into groups to avoid drawing attention to ourselves, although I don't think we succeeded. I stayed with the Whale, Boasnovas, and Erik the Belgian. The first thing we did was take a bath (well, four baths; one for each of us) and buy new clothes. Boasnovas chose a very elegant—if a bit showy—suit with lots of ribbons and adornments. And over his missing eye, he put on a black velvet patch edged in gold. Erik, however, bought simple clothes, much like what he had been wearing, but without stains or holes, and went to a barber to trim his enormous mustache.

I bought red boots, which I was very excited about, and some linen pants and a shirt, which were lightweight. And I cut my hair because, once I washed it, I saw that it hung down to my shoulders. For the Whale, a tailor had to sew two pairs of pants together to make one for him. And he fell in love with a bright blue jacket that was small on him (anyone could see that) but that he liked so much, so why rain on his parade. His shoulders were squeezed so tight, and his belly was so squished in, that he resembled a turquoise-colored sausage. I was worried that he couldn't breathe, but I consoled myself knowing that, in our next skirmish, the jacket would tear, putting an end to the problem. That jacket made the Whale so happy! Yes, it was best to let him enjoy shining like a hundred-kilo firefly for a few days—he had earned it.

At the time, none of us worried that the tailor was Chinese. And we weren't concerned when he turned pale—as if he'd seen a ghost—as soon as he saw the medallion around my neck. No, we didn't realize anything. We were too happily distracted. But you should take note: he was a very small Chinese man, with a face as wrinkled as parchment, bony hands, and a nose the size of a pea. I'll remind you of him later....

We agreed to meet up that night for dinner at L'Auberge de Sable (the Inn of Sand in French, Two Molars explained); he said it's useful to know different languages. We spent the first half hour laughing at how different we looked: elegant, clean-shaven, colorful, and gleaming. It was as if the circus had come to town. But the one who stole the show was One-Legged Jack when he walked in. He wore a hat with such large feathers that one couldn't see his face, and he was dressed in screamingly bright red balloon pants that cinched in at the knee, accentuating his new peg leg, made from ebony carved all around with grape leaves, clusters, and vines. Apparently, while passing by a furniture store, he fell in love with an Italian bed decorated from top to bottom, and he instructed the carpenter to make him a leg decorated just like the bed. It looked like he had swallowed an armchair and only a leg stuck out of him. It's like I told you before: pirates don't know what to do with their money.

Only Barracuda and Nuño looked like proper pirates still. The captain, freshly shaved, was dressed in his usual style, but in new, clean clothing. And Nuño, who as a young man must have been very handsome, looked like a rich nobleman. If he had driven through town in a carriage, people would have bowed when he went past; that's how distinguished he looked. The rest of us (let's be honest) looked like marionettes. We dined (but not too much) and drank nothing but water. We didn't have the strength left for anything else.

It must be said, in case you were wondering, that any of us could have retired with the riches we now had. But the thought never occurred to us. Aside from buying ourselves outlandish clothing, eating until we split our sides, leaving enormous tips in the inns, and covering ourselves in gold chains and earrings…

well, the truth is, we couldn't think of much else to do with the money. That's what pirates are like: always looking for treasures, to later keep looking for more treasures. That, without a doubt, is what they most enjoy doing.

"Well, Captain! In the end, it hasn't worked out badly at all, has it?" Two Molars asked, winking his eye as if a bug had flown into it. "Not bad at all for a consolation prize…"

"We must separate," Russian Kitty (dressed all in lilac) said from the end of the table, his voice very deep. "We are doomed! Fung Tao will chase us forever! Everyone knows that he swore to do so! After his ship exploded, his men pulled him from the sea. Right then he swore that, without ever resting, he would pursue whoever had his coffer! And on top of everything else, the

boy wears his medallion!" he exclaimed, pointing at my neck like someone looking at a ghost.

"Come now, Kitty," Jack interrupted him from behind the feathers of his hat, which he refused to remove even during dinner. "Those are just superstitions. No one knows whether he was ever in the Caribbean. Besides, in any event, Fung Tao must be wearing wooden pajamas by now…"

"Exactly!" Russian Kitty said, standing up. "He's…*dead*! And his ghost won't leave us in peace until…!"

"Silence!" Barracuda shouted from the other end of the table. "Have you all gone mad? Why don't you go out into the plaza and stop every passerby to tell them every detail, if you can find someone in this cursed archipelago who hasn't yet heard all about it with all your shouting!"

We fell silent. Despite not understanding our language,

the innkeeper seemed interested in our conversation. We were suddenly aware of his close presence, and it made us nervous. More than likely, though, it was all the shouting from our group of strangely dressed men that was what caught his attention.

"Let's go to Tortuga!" Malik proposed. "We could spend our money there without fearing that the English or the Spanish would take us prisoner. Now that area is a pirate zone! It would be like going on a holiday!"

"Captain," Erik said, standing up as if he were going to give a speech. "I...I have a theory that...I am almost certain that...," and he fell silent as if he were embarrassed.

"A theory?" Boasnovas remarked, seeing Erik hesitate. "He couldn't even read until just recently...and now he has theories!"

"Leave him alone, One-Eyed!" Nuño said. "Come on, Belgian, spit it out!"

"Well...maybe it's just silly, but..." Erik said, scrunching his eyebrows together as he thought really hard. "I strongly believe that Phineas' treasure really was in Kopra." He looked around at all of us. "Don't you all realize? When we found the book, it seemed to us like someone was pulling our leg, a joke in bad taste from old Krane, because we were expecting, gold, silver, and jewels. I mean, we didn't even know how to read then! But now I think that just because one might not know how to see the value of something, that doesn't mean it isn't a treasure...Look at all we've gotten since we found the book!"

"That's the truth," Boasnovas interrupted. "The you-know-what by you-know-whom has been a total success!" I think that he was winking his eye at us, but nobody realized it because he knew how to wink only the eye he was missing.

"He'll follow us until the end of time!" Russian Kitty moaned, but nobody paid attention.

"And not just that," I added. "It's not just money. Remember the refuge in the Cliffs of the Condemned!"

"That really saved our hides!" Malik exclaimed. "Although I shouldn't say so myself," he added, not wanting to boast..."And the ambush in Trinidad? If the Belgian hadn't remembered the story of Orson the Scot, they'd have given us a licking but good."

"Hey!" One-Legged Jack piped up. "Not all of us got out of that without a scratch, I'll remind you lot."

"In any event," the Whale said, "None of that is what's most important. Maybe what I'm about to say is pure foolishness, but I think the best part has been learning to read...Being able to understand what it says all over the place, of knowing what's inside a sack or a barrel without having to open it...Being able to listen to Phineas himself, even though he's no longer here or even if you had never met him! Before I knew how to read, I didn't know how many things I didn't know!"

"That's true, Whale!" I said. "And if you hadn't read that contract, then Bruno would've pulled a fast one over us but good!"

"Well..." the Whale replied, turning as red as a lobster. "That wasn't so important."

"What you're saying is not nonsense, Belgian," Nuño said in a low voice. Nuño looked at Barracuda, who remained motionless, facing forward, which was the most he did when he was in agreement with something.

"It's a pity," Nuño continued, "that old Krane didn't leave a map in the book that shows where all the riches he accumulated over the course of his life are stored. That would've been hitting the jackpot!"

"Well, that's what I was talking about," Erik said, also speaking softly. "I'm not so certain that Phineas' treasure map isn't in the book."

"Come on, Belgian," Two Molars said. "We've read it from front to back, and, yes, there is a lot of information about people, tricks, and characters of all sorts, but there is no map other than the one about you-know-who."

"We'll never be free of him!" the lilac-colored voice repeated. "Until the end of time!"

"Oh, pipe down, Kitty!" Malik suddenly shouted at him. "You're the most tiresome Russian I've ever met in my life!"

"Well, I think the map is there," Erik continued, "but it isn't a normal map, not one that's drawn, I mean..."

He put a finger to his lips and hissed at us to be quiet.

Then Erik stood up and unceremoniously placed his hands on the backs of the innkeeper and the bartender, and more or less by force accompanied them out onto the street.

"Well now, gentlemen," he said, "I'm pretty certain that you two don't understand us, but we want to be alone for just a little while, okay?" He closed the door and then he returned to his seat and continued speaking, much more excited now. "I think that the exact location of Phineas' treasure does appear in the book!"

"Explain yourself, Belgian," Barracuda said, taking part at last. "There are no maps in the book aside from the one about the coffer; I've already gone through it from cover to cover to check."

"Yes, Captain, I know it seems that way," the Belgian continued as if it hurt him to think. "But, what if we did find the key to Krane's treasure in Kopra. Just a key…made of paper… in the book."

We all looked at him. I don't mean to toot my own horn, but I began to understand what he was on about.

"Think about it, my friends," Erik continued. "The book was the perfect hiding place! If that crazy old man from Tortuga hadn't lost his head, what possibilities were there of someone finding that tiny island in the middle of the sea? Very few. And that it would be found by a pirate who knew how to read? Practically none! If Two Molars hadn't seen his name when he was flipping through the book, we would have left it there thinking it had no worth. But I think that Phineas left the clues to find his treasure written in the book, but not for just anyone; only those who were smart enough to spot them!"

"And you're the only one who's that clever?" Jack asked. "Because the rest of us haven't seen a thing…"

"Well, the truth is that I think I am," Erik said, shrugging his shoulders. "Everyone has looked for Krane's treasure on deserted islands, inaccessible cliffs, or the bottom of the sea— remote and difficult places to get to that have discouraged those who've tried. But if one is a pirate who knows exactly how his fellow pirates are, where would you hide it so that no one would find it?"

"I got lost back when you were talking about this map," the Whale said. "What kind of map isn't drawn?"

"Why, a map of words!" Erik the Belgian said, pulling out a sheet of paper. "Look here, I've copied some things from the book."

"Did you learn how to write?" John the Whale asked, his eyes growing very large.

"Well…once you know how to read, it's not so difficult. It's just a matter of trying."

"Wow!" the Whale said, and then looked at me. "Sparks, that's the next thing we need to learn how to do!"

"Now let's see," Erik began. "Fung Tao's treasure was the consolation prize for overcoming the two first obstacles: finding the book and reading it. But Krane left more clues for those who really paid attention to his words. Listen to this:

> "*A blind man can have the finest pearls in front of him and not see them. You can be sure that I shall hide my treasure far from the reach of the fiercest pirates. I've placed the key there where nobody could see it even if they found it. They would have it in front of their noses, and they wouldn't know how to see it; they couldn't decipher it.*

"Don't you see? The book is the key! They wouldn't know how to see it, Krane said! Because they wouldn't know how to read! And then there's this.

> "*The end of this pirate life of mine draws near. I want to retire, to rest and live peacefully in the place I've prepared for this moment, on the Miskito Coast. I've built there a house from where I can see the sea and spend my final days. I've prepared everything so that this is possible. There, waiting for me, guarded by a ghost, that which is most precious to me, that for which I have fought my entire life, and the peace of my old age.*"

"That's clear," Malik said, rubbing his bald head as if he were trying to polish it to a shine. "He retired to a place where he expects to have the peace that he's found so difficult to achieve. I don't see anything unusual about that."

"It doesn't say that," Erik corrected. "It says that waiting for him there is what *he has fought for his entire life* and *the peace of his old age*. Those are two separate things! Why has he fought for his entire life, and what is it that is 'most precious'? His treasure! Think about it, comrades: where do you hide something everyone is looking for? Why, right in front of their own noses!"

"By the devil!" Boasnovas said, his one eye as large as a plate, as he scanned the paper Erik had read. "I think the Belgian's on to something! In the past, we wouldn't have noticed a small detail like this, but it is true: it does say '*and.*' Those are two separate things!"

Barracuda stood up and rested his fist and his hook on the table.

"Are you telling me that Phineas Krane kept his treasure in his own house, on the Miskito Coast, the place most-crawling with pirates in the entire Caribbean? That's the most..." He looked at Erik as if he were going to gobble him up, but he didn't. "That's the most *fantastic* thing I've heard in my life! It's so absurd that it might even be true! Who would have guessed? What do you think, Nuño?"

It was only then that we noticed that Nuño was as purple as a plum and twisting his hands as if he were going to tear them off.

"What do I think?" he said furiously. "I'll tell you what I think! I think the Belgian is absolutely right! But let me tell you this: no one, and I repeat, *no one* is going to make me go back to the Miskito Coast!"

"He doesn't like to talk about it," Two Molars whispered. "Since that day he hasn't ever spoken his name."

We were back on board, and while Barracuda and Nuño had a shouting match in the captain's quarters, the rest of us were seated close together in the prow of the *Southern Cross*, as we did whenever something important happened. The night was full of stars; although it was late, nobody was tired. Our new clothes, however, were already worn and tired. Between the stench of the smoky lamps during dinner and the greasy remnants of food we dropped or wiped on ourselves, our fancy clothes now looked like our old attire. Some of us had even changed back into our old rags. The Whale, however, was still dressed in his too-tight turquoise jacket, even though some of the seams had begun to give under the pressure of his enormous bulk. My new red boots were already scuffed brown and black.

"Nobody knows what happened," Two Molars said, "and he's never told a soul. I just know that he never wanted to return to that place, populated by Miskito natives and a few Spaniards."

At that moment, the argument between the captain and Nuño rose in tone, and we heard Nuño shout, "I said no! Never! The sky will fall on my head, and sea monsters will start making pastries before I go back there! And I won't discuss it anymore! If you don't like it, you can leave me in Cartagena de Indias! I resign!"

"Enough, Nuño!" Barracuda roared. "We want you to come with us! Nobody knows those lands like you do! Besides, the… the crew needs you!"

"Never! Trees will grow upside down and waterfalls will flow upward before I go back there!"

"You're the stubbornest Spaniard I've ever met in my life!"

"No! I assure you, I'm not, Barracuda! The stubbornest, most despicable, traitorest Spaniard lives precisely on the Miskito Coast! That's why I won't go there!"

"By all that's holy, Nuño! But he's your brother!" yelled Barracuda.

On hearing this, we all stared at Two Molars, who nodded slowly. He was the only one of us who'd been part of the crew long enough to know this story. He spoke in a quiet voice.

"As far as I know, they came from Spain together when they were young men: Nuño and Rodrigo Mendoza, from Extremadura, arrived on these shores in search of their fortunes. They bought property in Portobelo, on the coast of Panama. That's where Barracuda and I met them. The captain was looking for a crew for the ship he had then, the *Celestial Star*, and enlisted both of them. They were formidable sailors! And swordsmen like you've never seen! Barracuda was very young then, but both the English and the Spanish Armadas already wanted his head. A good price they had put on it, just like now!

"One day, in a skirmish with some Portuguese merchants, we lost the *Star*. She sunk off the Jamaican coast, with no way to save her. It was a true disaster.

"Barracuda took it very hard and disappeared for almost a year. During that time, the Mendoza brothers set themselves up in Nicaragua, on the Miskito Coast. They were told that an ancient city full of gold and riches was in that area, and they were determined to find it. I didn't go with them because my place was on the sea, so I stayed in Portobelo to see if I could find another ship to sign on to. I heard many rumors about the two Spaniards: that they had found a solid gold statue that was three meters tall, that they had gotten lost in the jungle, that they had formed a musical theater company, and that they had been eaten by a giant crocodile. All lies, of course, but you know how people love to invent fantastical stories to surprise or scandalize other folk.

"Since I needed the money, I signed on to a fishing boat. Can you imagine that? Me, on a fishing boat! I didn't last very long, that's the truth, because the work was extremely hard; we had to get up really early to fish. And the smell of fish gets in your nose and then everything smells the same after a while. But before I gave up fishing, one day we dropped anchor off the Miskito Coast. We had been through a terrible storm and lost a few barrels of fresh water, so we landed to replenish our stocks. And you won't believe who we found in the middle of that desolate place! The two Spaniards!

"There the two of them were, in a cabin in the middle of nowhere, with their hair and beards long and their clothes torn, looking like shipwrecks. As soon as I saw them, I knew that things weren't good because they sat on opposite sides of the porch, and they didn't speak a word to one another the entire time we were with them. Nuño helped us fetch water from their cistern, and, when we'd finished, he asked the captain of the fishing boat if he could return to Portobelo with us. The captain accepted, and Nuño said 'Then let's go!' And that was that. I asked if he was

going to say goodbye to Rodrigo, who hadn't opened his mouth the entire time. Nuño looked at me and said: 'I don't have a brother!' Then he walked toward the ship without ever looking back.

"Once on the high seas, I tried to ask him what had happened between him and Rodrigo, but his only words were, 'Don't ever mention that name in my presence again.'

"Back in Portobelo, our paths crossed once again with Barracuda's, who had gotten another ship (our *Southern Cross*) and was in search of men. We signed on without thinking twice about it.

"Cleaned up, with a haircut and a shave, Nuño Mendoza, called since then Nuño the Spaniard, came on board as the second in command. He looked like a dashing hero. And that brings us to today. The rest of the story you all more or less already know."

When Two Molars finished his tale, the shouts from the captain's quarters had ceased. We remained in silence for a while. I wondered what could be so awful as to make two brothers stop talking to one another. I had never had a brother, but I was sure that I wouldn't last very long without even speaking to him because I'm a non-stop chatterbox. Besides…a brother, of all things! Who wouldn't want to have one? Why, I'd give half my freckles for one, even if he were small and weak.

I was lost in these thoughts when Nuño came out onto the deck. In the moonlight, his face was full of fury. We looked at him with pity, and that made him even angrier.

"I won't go!" he said firmly. "Fish will wear pigtails before I do! The desert will fill with frogs! I swear it!"

He went to the stern, alone, to look at the wake the ship left on the sea.

"Poor guy," said the Whale. "The words he's going to have to swallow when he finds himself on the Miskito Coast."

"Do you think he'll go?" I asked. "To me he looks pretty determined not to."

"He is very determined," the Whale replied. "I know him, and he never goes back on his word."

"Well then…?" I was confused.

My big friend looked at me, placed a hand on my shoulder, and gave me a big smile.

"It's like this, Sparks: I also know Barracuda!"

We set sail during the night, although the captain didn't shout out the destination as he normally did. I saw the men running from one side of the ship to the other between the sails and cords, but I was dead tired. I thought that perhaps I should get up and help. But maybe…yes, if they wanted me to do something, they would call me…In other words, I fell asleep before I could help it.

The sun awakened me around midday. We were on the open sea. I struggled to get up and went to see if I could do something: peel potatoes, swab the deck…the usual tasks that fell to me.

When I walked across the deck, I noticed the pirates looking upward, from time to time, out of the corners of their eyes. I looked upward as well but couldn't see anything. Boasnovas, his new eye patch already stained and lackluster, winked his remaining eye, trying to see something up in the sky.

"What's going on, Boasnovas?" I asked him. "Is a storm brewing?"

"A storm?" he replied. "No, no! We've got good weather for at least three days."

I kept walking and went searching for the Whale, who was coiling ropes in the stern.

"Hey, Whale! Do you know where we're going?"

"Yes, to the Miskito Coast."

"To the Mis…" I spluttered, with surprise. "And Nuño? The captain managed to convince him?"

"Convince him? No, I don't think so."

"Then, has he left the ship?"

"No. Nuño's coming as well," he replied, not giving it much importance.

"But…How…?"

Without pausing in his work, the Whale pointed upward, to

the top of the mainmast. At first, blinded by the sun, I couldn't see anything; but then I saw a lump in the crow's nest, at the top of the mast. I squinted and stared…It was the Spaniard, gagged and tied up like a parcel!

"I told you he'd come, Sparks," Whale said, without looking at me.

Two or three more hours passed. I did nothing but look upward, where Nuño journeyed against his will, wrapped up like an enormous silkworm cocoon on the ship's mast. He must be spitting mad! The day was scorchingly hot, but Barracuda waited until the afternoon was well advanced before coming out onto the deck and shouting, "Nuño! Have you got your wits back yet? If you promise to be reasonable, I'll set you loose!"

Nuño didn't answer (the truth is, he couldn't because he was gagged), but the noises that came from up above left no doubt that he hadn't changed his mind.

"Well," the captain replied. "If that's what you want, that's how it'll be. You'll stay there until you can be reasonable again!" Then Barracuda said to me, "Sparks, climb up there and give him some water and a bit of food. I don't want to reach the Miskito Coast with the cadaver of a Spaniard tied to the mainmast…"

And he left. The rest continued with their tasks as if everything were normal. I was in disbelief. I went down into the pantry and got cheese, bread, a bit of jerky, and a jug of water. I put it all in a sack, which I hung over my shoulder, and I climbed the rigging that led to the top of the mast.

When I arrived, Nuño's eyes were shooting flames. On seeing me, he got so restless that I thought he would burst the cords that bound him. He was inside the crow's nest but tied to the mast like a suckling pig about to be thrust into the oven. Believe me when I say that I was a bit afraid to approach him to remove the rag from his mouth, but I did it. Right away, because it was blisteringly hot, I gave him some water. I held the jug up to his mouth, and he drank the entire thing in one gulp. But as soon as the water passed through his gullet, he started shouting like a madman.

"Untie me, Sparks! Come on! I order you! When I get down from here, more than one person is going to wish they'd never been born! You'd better believe me! You won't make me go there!"

And he didn't say anything more because I, who didn't know what to do, put the gag back in his mouth so he would shut up.

"Come on, Nuño, calm down…You know that I can't…Do you want some cheese? I've also brought a bit of jerky…" But he was so angry that he wouldn't stop screaming, even though I couldn't understand what he was saying. "He can't be that terrible, man! After all, he's your brother!"

Then he got *really* angry. It looked like he might swallow the gag, he was so furious. Feeling guilty—I don't know why—I left the cheese and bread beside him and hurried down as fast as I could.

That wasn't a good idea, I later realized. One, because tied up like that, he couldn't eat; and two, because the rest of the day, while the food lasted, the seagulls used poor Nuño as a toilet. The journey to the Miskito Coast was long, and Nuño spent it in the same place. Every time we tried to untie him, he threatened to throw himself overboard or to do terrible things to the rest of us. So he spent the entire crossing up there. We put a hat on him, he ate little, drank just enough, and by the time we arrived, the

veins of his forehead were so swollen that it looked like he'd had a serpent tattooed onto it.

We arrived at last, but not even after mooring the ship could we let Nuño loose. As soon as we took away the gag, he let loose with such loud cussing that our ears were almost bleeding, so we had to muzzle him once more. When we disembarked, we thought to bring him along with just his hands tied together, but as soon as his feet touched the ground, he began to run toward the sea with such determination that he was about to drown himself a few times. I can assure you that never, neither before nor after, had I seen Nuño so out of himself. Now that I think of it, not he nor anyone else. Ever. One might have thought that he had swallowed ten rats with toothaches and that they were gnawing on his entrails from inside him. And so the Whale hoisted up Nuño and tied him onto his back, facing backward as if he were the Whale's knapsack. A really angry knapsack, that is.

We walked down a long stretch of beach. Russian Kitty, who didn't want to be there either, was last in line, looking all around as if an infantry battalion might attack at any moment. The beach soon ended at the edge of a jungle. The vegetation was so thick, choking out the daylight, that it seemed as if night had fallen. We found a path that led through the jungle, and we followed it for a while. Suddenly, it opened onto a clearing, where there was an enormous house. Over the door, a sign read: "The Galleon. Food and Lodging." The inn looked as if it were empty, but that was about to change since fifty-three guests had suddenly turned up: the entire crew of the *Southern Cross*.

I'll tell you, in case you didn't already know, that fortune can be inexplicably capricious. Sometimes you can search for someone your entire life and never find them. Other times, however, although you don't want to run into that certain someone, and you hide beneath the largest rock in the middle of the farthest desert, you'll run into him. Both situations are equally certain to take place.

And that's precisely what happened in this case. The Miskito Coast is more than four hundred kilometers long and seventy wide, and, nonetheless, there, in the middle of nowhere, more than fifteen years later and without any warning, whom do you think we found behind the counter of the Galleon?

Exactly!

It wasn't necessary for anyone to say anything because the innkeeper was an exact copy (and I mean exact) of our Nuño. It was as if Nuño had arrived there ahead of us! He even had the same mustache!

Everyone was astonished; well, everyone except the captain and Two Molars, who in unison said (as if it were the most normal thing in the world), "Oh, hadn't I mentioned? They're twins."

Barracuda stepped forward. "Hola, Rodrigo! What a surprise to find you here! It's been ages!"

"A long time, Captain," the Spaniard answered (the other Spaniard, that is; not *ours*).

"The truth is, we didn't know if we would find you. We could use your services."

"Well, Barracuda, I left pirating behind years ago. This inn is more boring, but it's also more peaceful. And today you have it all to yourselves! Some lumberjacks have just left, and the rooms are vacant; you can stay as long as you like."

"No, it's not that," Barracuda clarified, "although it would also be good for us to rest here today. We're looking for a place, and you, who must know this area better than anyone, could perhaps guide us there. The other guide we have doesn't seem to be very interested in helping us…I'll pay you well."

"If it's just that…" Rodrigo replied. "I can do it. I know this jungle as if I had planted it myself…I'll take you wherever you need to go."

The captain remained quiet for a moment.

"Before anything else," he said at last, "I think it is fair that you should know that with us is…"

He made a sign to the Whale, who turned around. When the

two Spaniards were face to face, they seemed to be looking in a mirror inside a nightmare: one, frozen while he ran a cloth over the countertop; the other, tied up like a bundle on the back of a giant. The two of them turned bright red at the same moment, which was even stranger, and they glared at one another with such intensity that I thought they would make their heads explode simultaneously.

"So you've come back…" Rodrigo said slowly. "Well, well! Of all the holes of the Caribbean, I knew that someday you'd come back to fall into mine!"

"It wasn't voluntary," Whale said, his voice sounding funny because his back was still turned, and he shook Nuño like a puppet.

Erik elbowed him, and the Whale muttered, "Well, it's not like he can say anything himself!"

"We'll see," the captain said, approaching Nuño and removing the gag from his mouth. "If there's one place where we can be one-hundred-percent certain that you'll keep quiet, it's right here!"

Sure enough, Nuño didn't say a word. Nobody said anything for a very looooong and tenssssse moment.

"Well, brother," Rodrigo the innkeeper said at last. "I'd be delighted for you to stay here in my residence. Perhaps, for lunch. I'll prepare for you…a *paella*."

Oh my! This was when everything went mad! Just hearing about the food made our Nuño suffer a kind of fit of fury like I've never seen before! He began to twist around as if his underwear were full of gunpowder. He twisted so much that, although you wouldn't believe it if you hadn't seen it for yourself, he wound up knocking the Whale to the floor. The worst part is that Nuño fell underneath him, and the weight of our enormous Whale almost squashed him. We turned the Whale over, and Barracuda pulled out his dagger and cut the cords that bound the Spaniard. Then Barracuda grabbed him by the neck of his shirt, lifted him to his feet and walked outside with him. He backed Nuño up against a palm tree and all of us, crowded into the doorway, heard this conversation between the two of them:

"Now, look here, Nuño," Barracuda said, placing his hands on his hips. "This stopped being funny a long time ago. You're acting like a child. Whatever it was that happened, it was fifteen years ago! Besides, he's your twin brother, for crying out loud!"

"I won't forgive him! Never! Not even if my entrails are tied around my ears!" Nuño answered, huffing like a buffalo. "Didn't you hear him? Didn't you hear?"

"Didn't I hear *what*? You're acting like a complete lunatic!" The captain tried to calm down. He took a deep breath, rested his hook on the palm tree, right next to Nuño, and continued with a calmer voice. "Look, I don't know what happened between the two of you. I'm not your father; I won't give you the whole speech about Rodrigo being your own blood or that family is what's most important. No, I won't do that. I know that you're a reasonable man, the most reasonable of any I know; that's why you're my second in command. I'm sure you have your reasons for not wanting anything to do with Rodrigo. But listen to me well, Spaniard. I could care less if you make peace with him or not. I've come here for just one thing: Krane's treasure. Neither you nor your brother nor all the Spaniards of the Armada are going to get in my way. You can bet my right hand you won't!" He showed Nuño his hook. "And, as you can see, I've already given my left…"

Nuño seemed to calm down. I can assure you that when

Barracuda gets serious like this, anyone's knees would grow weak.

"Reasons?" came the high voice of Rodrigo, who was also watching the scene from the door of the inn. "Tell him why you got mad, Nuño, go on…"

"I don't want to talk to you!" Nuño said, still leaning against the palm tree. "Captain, please, get him out of my sight!"

"Fifteen years! He's been mad for fifteen years because… Why don't you tell him, brother?"

"He's the one…I mean, he's the *only* one who's angry?" I asked Rodrigo. "Not you as well?"

"Me?" he asked. "Please! Why should I be angry over something so trivial? He's the one who stopped talking to me… to this very day!"

"How could I?!" Nuño said, turning and moving toward us. "How could I tolerate something like that? Do you want to know what happened? Do you really want to know what this heartless piece of meat did to me? Fine! I'll tell you! It took me days to get everything required. I had to bribe the captain of a merchant ship to get some of the things…I did it all for him! For this selfish vermin who calls himself my brother! And after, when it was over, did he thank me? Nooo! Did he think of all the work I'd done for him? Nooo, sir!"

"But what the heck are you talking about, Nuño?" Erik asked from within the group of us crammed in the doorframe.

"Yes, go on…tell them, go on!" Rodrigo interjected, smiling from ear to ear as he leaned against the inn.

"That's not important!" Nuño went on, whirling his arms around. "What's important is that you acted like a royal ba…"

"A paella," Rodrigo interrupted him, without changing his posture.

There was silence.

"A…paella?" Barracuda asked, walking toward us from behind Nuño.

"Yes," the innkeeper replied. "I told him it was too salty."

I, who had known him for three years now, had never seen the captain so surprised. If a crocodile were to speak to him one night from beneath his own bed, I doubt if his face would have been like it was just then. He looked at Nuño as if he didn't know him, but Nuño just kept on with his story.

"I spent all morning making it! The kitchen was hotter than the bowels of a volcano! And I did it only because you said that you missed the food from Spain! And did you thank me? Noooo! You acted like an ungrateful, selfish cretin!"

"All this is…over a paella?" Boasnovas said, unbelieving.

"I don't understand. What is it?" the Whale asked. "I've never heard of a 'paella' before in my life!"

"It's a rice dish," Rodrigo explained.

"Don't say it like that!" Nuño said, without calming down. "If you say it like that, it sounds like it's something ridiculous!"

"Rice?" One-Legged Jack asked. "All of this bother is over some rice?"

"Rice," whimpered the Kitty. "It's the Chinese pirate! The Curse!"

"Oh, for heaven's sake!" Malik said to the Russian. "I liked you more when you didn't open your mouth."

"It can't be," I said. "Nuño would never do something so… so "

"Say it, lad," Rodrigo intervened. "So stupid!"

"Well, the mystery is unveiled," Boasnovas said. "Some stories certainly are better if you don't know all the details."

"I don't expect for you lot to understand!" Nuño exclaimed, still angry. "That's asking too much. Said like that: 'a plate of rice' makes it all sound absurd. But you don't know what…"

Barracuda pushed Nuño out of his way (and Nuño suddenly fell quiet), waved the rest of us out of the way, and headed toward the door of the inn. He stopped just before entering and, without turning around, said very slowly: "I don't want to hear another word about this…matter. I won't lose a single second more on this. Rest today. Rodrigo, tomorrow we'll leave early to find what we've come here looking for. There won't be any further distractions."

We looked at Nuño as if we didn't know him, and he looked back at us as if he couldn't believe that we didn't support him.

"You just don't understand," he spluttered. "You can't under…"

"Come on, Nuño!" John the Whale cut him short. "I admire you…but this is about rice! Even I can see that this is just silly!"

We left Nuño outside, all alone, and the rest of us went inside to eat something. We barely spoke during the meal because we were all shocked by what had happened. None of us could have thought that Nuño—the most sensible of all, always so calm, the one who never got upset and rarely raised his voice—might also make mistakes and commit a ludicrous folly of this degree. After that day, we often told the story of the Spaniards and the paella, and everyone who heard it thought it was too incredible or an outright lie.

The next morning we set out very early—almost before dawn. Rodrigo told us that he could find the place where Phineas had built his house. Many rumors ran along the coast, and they all pointed to the same area. Because of what the book said, we thought we would find it on a beach facing the sea, with the sand reaching the door to the house. But no, things aren't that easy, at least not for pirates.

The path Rodrigo showed us was very narrow. The day was stiflingly hot, but we never stopped during our ascent of slopes so muddy that we slipped a thousand times. All of our new finery (well, it was no longer that fine) that we'd bought in Basse-Terre was now even worse because it was covered in muck.

From the moment we left the inn, nobody mentioned Nuño. In the years that followed, the paella story became legendary in taverns throughout the Caribbean. At least a thousand different versions—and I know because I've heard them all—were told about what happened to Nuño during those days: that he disappeared forever and his soul thirsting for vengeance wanders the Miskito Coast; that he burned down the inn as soon as we left it; and that he challenged his brother to a duel on the beach and killed him with a shout of "It wasn't salty!" And still another tale claimed that Barracuda tied him to a pole, covered in pig's fat, and left him for the crows…In short, all lies. I'll tell you what really happened.

We had walked for more than half a day when Erik the Belgian overtook the Whale and me, whispering to us in a low voice, "We're being followed, my friends."

We looked back and saw Nuño crawling behind us on his hands and knees. He also saw us but didn't say a word. For the entire afternoon, he followed some distance behind us. Feeling tremendous pity for him, I moved forward along our line and reached Rodrigo, who was in the lead with Barracuda.

"Rodrigo…Your brother is following behind—"

"I know," he interrupted me. "I saw him this morning as soon as we left. Leave him; he needs a lesson."

Barracuda, at his side, didn't even open his mouth. One never knew what that man was thinking. I had always thought that he and Nuño were friends, but there you had it; it was as if he couldn't care less about the Spaniard's fate, as if it was all the same to him if he slipped off one of those steep embankments or got swallowed up by some ten-foot-long python.

The journey (as always) was extremely difficult. I don't know why people think that a pirate's life is simple and comfortable. Nothing is further from the truth. This business of searching for treasure and attacking ships is exhausting. Even if you are lucky and avoid injury in an attack or a skirmish, your feet are always hurting, your hands are scraped raw by the ropes, and it's almost impossible to sleep through an entire night. And that's if you don't get seasick! That's the worst. All of us have been seasick at one time or another. For some, at first, it happens when they're a sprog, a brand-new pirate on board a ship for the first time; for others, it hits at any moment and without warning because of a storm or because on that particular day, they're not in hearty shape. One's innards get all twisted up, and you wind up feeding the fish everything you've ever eaten, back to the first mother's milk you had as a babe.

So, now you can appreciate how hard a pirate's life is and how demanding our journey was on that day. We trudged through extreme conditions all day long: mud, relentless heat, poisonous insects and critters, and dangerous terrain. By the time the sun began to set, I was dying from exhaustion. We set up camp for the night in the middle of nowhere. We unrolled our mats to sleep on, lit a bonfire to keep wild animals at bay, and ate. There was no moon; the night sky closed in on us like a dark cave. I couldn't stop thinking that out there, somewhere far from our fire, alone and angry, was poor Nuño. How awful pride is!

I saw that many of the pirates also peered into the darkness, surely thinking the same as I was. But not Barracuda. He stared right into the flames; the fire reflected in his eyes and seemed to draw gold doubloons in them. If he was worried, I can assure you that nobody would have guessed it.

I didn't sleep well at all. I dreamed that I was being swallowed by a frog whose mouth was full of lava. I ran, but its long tongue caught me again and again. I sweated buckets as I slept.

The Whale woke me with a jab of his elbow. I was about to complain, but then he pointed toward the end of the slope where we had camped. A little apart from us, almost at the edge of a cliff and silhouetted against the morning mist, Nuño and Rodrigo were talking in low voices, their arms crossed.

We couldn't hear what they were saying. First, Rodrigo spoke while Nuño nodded his head. And then the opposite. The other pirates were waking up and also kept silent as we watched the two Spaniards speaking to one another. At one point, they both fell silent, facing one another, just staring at each other for what seemed an eternity to me. Suddenly, as if someone had given a signal, they hugged one another and started slapping each other affectionately on the back. As they headed back toward us, we all looked at one another as if we were embarrassed.

The brothers approached the camp as companions, each with his arm over the other's shoulders. Our Nuño looked like a true gentleman: clean, well-combed, with his leather jacket and his sword at his belt. No one would guess that he'd spent a day crawling through the muck; he was elegant, even in the middle of the filthiest jungle. At his side, his copy (Rodrigo) was so scruffy, disheveled and dirty, that together they looked like the same person before and after being trampled by a herd of buffalos.

"In three hours, the heat will be unbearable," Barracuda said from behind us. "We've got to get going now. Nuño! Get this troop of layabouts moving!"

And everything went back to normal. This was the captain's only and very peculiar way of saying that he was glad that Nuño had returned to us: without saying anything, acting as if nothing had happened, and never speaking of it again. But as we got underway, we couldn't help but notice that, whether or not we found Phineas' treasure, our journey had served an important purpose: to reunite two brothers who hadn't seen one another for some fifteen years. For people like us (most without families), having a brother was something like hitting a jackpot, and I know that we all secretly envied the two Spaniards. After their reconciliation, everything between them was, "Whatever you say," "No, you first," or "I'm sure you're right." After fifteen years of disagreement, they had to balance things out with a whole lot of agreement.

Rodrigo led us deeper and higher into that jungle full of palm trees. Although everyone was an adult (except for me, of course), some pirates (and when I say *some*, I mean *the Whale*) repeatedly asked: "Are we there yet?"

We were exhausted, and pirates, when we're tired, always fall into a foul mood. So when the Russian Kitty, soaked with sweat, as if he had been swimming in the ocean, said, "I think we should turn around before it's too late. The curse—" he couldn't finish. Because Boasnovas, who was almost always in a good mood, threw himself on top of him and pushed the Russian's face into

the mud while shouting, "Shut up! By all the skeletons in the deep sea, shut up! Or I'll go mad! I'm fed up with this nonsense about the Fung Tao, the coffer, the curse…and you! Above all, with you, you tiresome whiner!"

We had to separate them because otherwise Boasnovas might've burst a vein in his neck with all his shouting. Just then, we heard Rodrigo cry out from the head of the line, "There! There it is! I knew it!"

And sure enough: right in front of us, on the top of a hill, in a sunny green clearing there was…the home of Phineas Krane! It was a large and lovely dwelling. And although it wasn't on a beach, it had a breathtaking view of the sea. The house was made of stone, with an enormous porch and doors big enough for a man to enter on horseback. It looked like the house of a Marquis, but it was abandoned, and the jungle had begun to devour it. Plants had sprouted in the cracks between the stones, between the steps, under the door, and around the windows. Without a doubt, old Krane had picked a pretty place in which to retire, but fate (or bad luck) had decided he would never live here, not even for one day.

"We're not so clever, my friends…" Erik the Belgian said. "It looks like someone has beaten us here."

The doors looked as if they'd been forced open. One of them was hanging off its hinges, and several windows were wide open.

Barracuda huffed in disgust and went right up to the door. He sunk his hook into the wood and pulled it open. We entered in silence. The entryway opened onto a large room full of dark wood furniture, various sofas, and, on the wall opposite the door, a fireplace as large as a man. Everything was destroyed: the furniture knocked over, the curtains torn, broken plates on the floor…A thick layer of dust covered every surface, obscuring any color. It looked as if the house had been looted many times and that thieves had broken whatever didn't seem valuable to them.

We remained silent.

"If there were anything here," Rodrigo said, "surely it would have been found…"

Suddenly, someone shouted. We turned immediately toward the source; it was the Kitty, even paler than his normal white-as-snow paleness. His hands covered his mouth, and his eyes looked ready to fall out of their sockets as he stared at the wall at the back of the room. There, above the fireplace, were two symbols written in red upon the white wall.

"What the heck are those scribbles?" I asked.

"I didn't see those in the book...Are those letters?" John the Whale asked. "Does anyone know what it says?"

"Yes," the Russian answered slowly. "I've seen those symbols before...They're Chinese letters. They spell *Fung Tao!* He has been here!"

All the valerian root in the world couldn't have calmed the Russian Kitty's nerves. He trembled as if he had been tied to an oxcart going over a cobblestone road. The rest of us were also rather worried, to tell the truth. It wasn't that we were afraid…Well, a little bit, why deny it. I'm not superstitious, but…You've got to understand what the situation was: we reached an uninhabited place in the very middle of the Miskito Coast, and there we found the sign of the dead Fung Tao whose cursed coffer full of valuable stones we'd stolen…Well, I don't know about you, but it did spook me just a little bit. I'd even say that the dragon medallion began to feel heavy around my neck…

But then, that's why we had with us Barracuda, the bravest and most-feared pirate of the entire Caribbean!

"Worthless wimps!" Barracuda roared. He then continued in such a loud voice that it shook the house. "I've come here for Phineas Krane's treasure, and I'm not leaving without it. So if anyone dead or alive has anything to say, let them say it now."

He waited a very short moment, but it was long enough for the hairs to stand on end all over our bodies. We responded with silence.

"Do you see?" the captain said. "This is all just foolishness! Nuño, are you coming?" And he went to inspect the house further.

We could see it in his face that Nuño wasn't at all happy with this. But after the incident with the paella, he wasn't in any position to be finicky. The rest of us remained petrified in the living room, as still as statues. Well, all except for the Russian Kitty and One-Legged Jack, who tried to hold the Kitty down, and, as a result, trembled as much as he did, making his wooden leg go tock tock tock on the floor as if it were a drum. Suddenly, all of us leaped into the air, startled because a voice came from out of the darkness, "Come on, you water rats. I didn't bring you all this way for you to faint like damsels! Start searching this wretched place!" Barracuda roared.

To say that we moved slowly would be an exaggeration. A sleepy bag of snails would've moved faster than we did. There were at least five bedrooms, a kitchen, a bathroom, and something that might have been a library in that house. Nothing was left standing in any of the rooms.

But as we had made such a long and arduous journey to get there, we had to give it a try. I must say that searching, opening drawers, and looking under mattresses is like scratching an itch— once you start, you can't stop. As you'll understand, fifty-four pirates (I've counted Rodrigo among us here) searching through an abandoned house make a considerable racket, and I won't even talk about the clouds of dust we raised.

After a good while, we were exhausted, covered in a fine layer of white dust, and convinced that nothing of any value remained there.

"There isn't even any loose change here, Captain," Jack sighed. "We've searched for hiding places even in the walls and floors themselves, and nothing! If the treasure were ever here, someone took it already."

"That can't be!" Barracuda responded angrily. "If someone had found Phineas' treasure, I would have heard about it. Who could keep something like that a secret?"

"I must not be as clever as I thought…" Erik said, crestfallen. "I've brought you all here for a stupid idea that…I'm sorry, Captain! I'm an idiot!"

"Don't say that!" the Whale told him. "It was a good theory. And look how good it turned out for the two Spaniards!"

A long time had passed since we had found ourselves in a similar situation: there on the island of Kopra, when we couldn't find Krane's treasure either; although, we did find the book that changed our lives forever. It now seemed as if that had been a century ago; we had changed so much since then!

I started to think that old Phineas had given us the slip twice now. He was a brilliant fellow. But we also owed him for having learned to read and for learning to look at things with fresh eyes since not everything that was valuable seemed so at first. Believe me, this is one of the best lessons I can give you: don't judge anything or anyone too quickly because you run the danger of making a serious mistake.

"Come on!" Nuño said, with resolution. "There's nothing for us here, and the way back is long!"

Without a doubt, everything might have ended there. We would have continued our lifestyle of attacking and boarding ships, and Phineas Krane's treasure would have been a thorn in the captain's heart (if he had one). But serving on the crew of the cleverest pirate of the Caribbean has its advantages....

Most of us had already left the house when Barracuda ran back inside, stood in the middle of the living room, and shouted, "Belgian! Read to me again what it says in the book about this house!"

Erik, who was already outside like I was, looked at us without understanding. Even so, he pulled out the wrinkled piece of paper he carried in his bag and went back inside. And of course, the rest of us followed him.

"A blind man might have before him the finest pearls and not see them," Erik read. *"You can be sure that I'll hide my treasure far from the reach of the fiercest pirates. I've left the key there—"*

"No," the captain interrupted him, "later on! Before the bit about peace and old age."

The Belgian looked at him, then searched through the words on the page to read aloud:

"I've built there a house from where I can see the sea and spend my final days. I've prepared everything so that this is possible. There, waiting for me, guarded by a ghost, that which is most precious to me, that for which I have fought my entire life, and the peace of my old age."

"EXACTLY!" Barracuda shouted.

He approached the fireplace and sunk his hook into the wall with a tremendous thunk. The metal sunk into the wall, right in the middle of the name of Fung Tao. The Russian all but fainted.

"It's happened to him again…" the Whale whispered beside me. "The madness he got in Kopra."

But Barracuda pulled out his hook and gave the wall another blow, sinking into it as if it were butter.

"'Guarded by a ghost,'" he explained, turning back toward us. "Don't you understand?"

"Well, I'll be tarred and feathered!" Nuño said, his eyes as big as saucers. "Of course! A ghost! Fung Tao has never been here. It was Phineas, curse him, who left those signs to frighten away the gullible!"

Nuño wrenched off the leg of an upside-down sofa and started to beat on the wall. The Whale, Erik, and I joined him with what we could find on the floor. It's not that I did all that much to enlarge the hole, but as I've said before, I like to be in the middle of everything. It was the Whale who, with a single blow of his fist, almost knocked down the fireplace.

After sailing without rest to every corner of this emerald sea, after Kopra, after being fired and re-hired, after Bruno, Orson, and the fight in Trinidad, after the reconciliation of the paella, and after so much search and searching for it…There it was! The magnificent, brilliant, enormous treasure of Phineas Johnson Krane! Even if I wrote a hundred pages, I couldn't list for you how many jewels, how many gold and silver coins, vessels, and chains there were. No pirate had ever seen so much priceless treasure—valuable beyond belief!

What happened afterward, we promised not to say. It was an agreement that the crew made among ourselves, even though the captain didn't ask us to. We did it because we knew that it would destroy his reputation of being a heartless pirate. But, since a long time has now passed, I think that I will tell you.

Barracuda began to skip around the room as if his feet were burning. None of us could know that, in reality, he thought he was dancing. Try to understand: he was a fierce and serious man, and I think that it was the very first time he had ever tried to dance. Afterward, as if we weren't surprised enough, he went around and gave a loud kiss on the forehead to each and every one of us. I don't know if we were more astonished by the treasure or by the captain's acting this way. Some reached up to feel their foreheads as if they'd been shot by a musket; I nearly split my sides laughing.

If ever I saw a pirate who was hard as flint be happy, have no doubt, it was on that day. I am sure that it wasn't just because of the riches (which were enormous, as I've already said), but because, at last and after many years, Barracuda, the most feared and admired captain of the Caribbean, had defeated another legendary pirate: Phineas Krane. It was like deposing the old king and winning the throne, all at the same time.

You and I have come a long way together, without a doubt. You've been incredible company on this story's journey: loyal and brave. I couldn't have asked for more. And now that we're nearing the end, I feel sad to be leaving all of you. I hope that you don't forget me and that, when you find yourself in some trouble, you'll remember that there's always a way out of it: sometimes, with what you know; other times, thanks to a friend; and then perhaps with a bit of help from good luck!

What happened after that memorable day still fills the stories that are told on the star-filled nights in the Caribbean. Fifty-four pirates (because Rodrigo became one of us) who were happy and rich set anchor in Tortuga. In case you were wondering, I'll tell you: no, we didn't split up. We were the closest thing to a family that any of us had. Nor did we leave the *Southern Cross*. It was even more incredible than that....

THE END (OR NOT)

The Whale and I, all dressed up and with a bag full of money, decided to go ashore in Tortuga before the *Southern Cross* sailed on. We had a week of something that could be called "leave." The Whale had made up his mind to grow a ridiculous tiny mustache that was like a line of ants walking single file beneath his nose. He was the only one who thought it made him look like he wasn't a pirate anymore, but I didn't want to argue with him.

We wandered the city until we came to a little shop in a back street, outside of which hung a sign that read "Books and Paper." We opened the door and froze in shock. There were piles of books from floor to ceiling, of every size and color imaginable! You, who are people who read, have undoubtedly visited more than one bookstore, but neither the Whale nor I had ever seen so much paper all in one place.

"Oh my, Sparks, all the books in the world must be here!"

"That's what it would seem, Whale," I answered. I now know that wasn't the case; the world has so many more books. But we couldn't even imagine that back then, of course.

"And how are we going to choose which one to get?" the enormous pirate with the tiny mustache asked. "Even if we spend all week looking at them, how could we decide?"

"Were you looking for something in particular?" a very sweet voice asked us from behind an enormous pile of books. "You can ask me anything you want. It looks like there's no order here, but I know where everything is."

From behind the mahogany counter came a tiny old woman with large eyeglasses and white hair pulled back in a bun. She wore a black and gray dress with a neat little apron. She looked like someone's charming grandmother.

"Well…You see, ma'am," I began to say. "The thing is, we would like to buy a few books and—"

"Then you're in the right place, gentlemen!" the old woman interrupted me, grabbing books from here and there from around the shop. "What are you looking for? Books of poetry? Novels? Theater? Comedies, tragedies…*adventures*?"

"Oh my," the Whale said again, under his breath. "We'll never get out of here! We can't decide!"

The old woman grabbed her chin with her thumb and index finger. Then, suddenly, she started to rush here and there like a spinning top, and she handed me book after book, each one heavier than the one before.

"Well, I'd recommend that you read *Amadis of Gaul*, for knights and adventures, and also *The Adventures of Marco Polo*, which is full of exotic places and incredible things, in far-away China."

"We won't let the Russian Kitty get ahold of that one," the Whale whispered in my ear, and I had an attack of giggles. "He'd have a heart attack! He still wakes up shouting some nights…"

"Aha!" the bookseller continued, still going about her business. "And this one here! It just came in recently, but they say it's a big success over in Spain! *Don Quixote of La Mancha*. It's in two volumes, and I have both of them…"

"Spain!" the Whale said, looking at the book the woman had handed him. "That's where Nuño and his brother are from! I've heard a lot about Spain…Almost all the boats loaded with gold head there!"

"Are these gifts then? Any of these would be a good gift," the woman said.

"No…they're not gifts," I said, but the Whale interrupted me.

"Actually, they are! Your birthday is coming up, isn't it, Sparks?"

"My…My birthday? Well…yes!" I said, and the hair on the back of my neck stood on end. I didn't really know when I had been born, but now we celebrated it on the day that Nuño had found me on Española.

"We'll have a party, Sparks!" the Whale decided. "With a pumpkin tart and everything. Twelve-years-old is an important age! Let me get them for you as a gift…We'll take all of them!" he told the old woman, picking up all four books. "What do we owe you, ma'am?"

"All four? Very good, that's a wonderful gift!" She began to add up the bill. "Let's see…One plus two…plus another two… That will be two doubloons and one escudo."

"Just two and a half?" the Whale said, surprised, as he looked at the books he held in his hand. "Wow, how inexpensive! And with what it must cost to write one of these! Not to mention the ink and the paper, and some quills to write with."

The bookseller took the books again and made a lovely package, wrapping them in a red cloth and tying it up with a blue bow. We gave her the money and left the bookstore, with my gift under one arm.

"Two and a half!" John kept repeating. "I think I've never bought anything so cheap! Look at all the words these books have! You'll let me read them, won't you, Sparks?"

I don't think I even answered him. I was very worried. I had then an enormous secret, one of the biggest kind…I didn't like to keep secrets, especially from my good friend John the Whale, but I was afraid to tell it.

And you'll have to forgive me, but I won't tell it to you just yet either….

Anyway, all of that worry abrubtly ceased once we were back

outside. The sun was shining fiercely, and in the distance, we could hear loud thuds. As we left the city and approached the sea, the sounds grew in intensity. Any pirate would have recognized those sounds. They were the sounds of cannon fire! What's more, even though at the time I thought I was hallucinating, I saw a tiny, old Chinese man with a wrinkled face and a nose as small as a pea running away from behind a bale of hay that was stacked near the street…Do you remember the tailor of Basse-Terre? I told you so!

We picked up our pace, growing more alarmed with every step. As we reached the street that led to the port, the noise became deafening. And when we reached the pier where we had anchored a week before, what we saw left us speechless.

If I've ever felt true fear, I can say that it was on that day. Still tied to the dock, the *Southern Cross* was burning at its prow with flames that were like tongues of fire. The crew was struggling to loosen the ship's moorings, attempting to head out to sea, where they could defend themselves. The Whale, in two great leaps, reached the ship and untied the ropes attached to the prow, which were burning without breaking. Then he turned to me and shouted something I couldn't understand. I was unable to move. Then he ran back toward me, threw me over one shoulder and carried me to some barrels. He stuck me inside of one and gave me the package of books.

"Sparks!" he shouted over the noise of the explosions. "Hide yourself! You've got the money, right? Don't move from here until we've left!"

"But…What are you saying?" I protested. "No! I'm going with you!"

"No, you're not!"

Close by, a cannon shot sounded. The wood from our ship splintered all around us. John the Whale grabbed me by my shoulders and said, staring intently into my eyes:

"This is serious, boy! Stay here, in Tortuga, and I can find you! I…I've got to go, but I promise I'll come back for you! I promise!" And then enormous Whale, with his eyes full of tears, made an X with his finger over the middle of his chest and spat onto the ground. "May I be eaten by hungry sharks if I don't!"

That's how my friend left, running without looking back even once. I saw him leap onto the burning ship just as it pulled away from the dock, sailing straight toward the enemy and firing at it without mercy.

And I remained on land.

Almost without realizing it, I squeezed the medallion hanging around my neck in one hand.

There on the other side of the estuary, near the port, a blackened bamboo ship with patched and faded red sails bobbed in the waves like a ghost. It was the *Dragon's Blood*, without a doubt; Fung Tao's ship that Phineas Krane had attacked in the distant seas of China.

And my pirate friends, with brave Barracuda as their leader, were going to meet them without me. That's how things can change in life: while you're distracted thinking about other things.

If we talk of Barracuda's treasure, we should stop right here: with me alone, inside a barrel, holding a red package of books tied with a blue bow. For here is where my first stage as a pirate ends, at the tender age of almost twelve-years-old.

Of course, if you're wondering what happened afterward... Well, that's another story! You wouldn't believe it either!

Maybe someday I'll tell it to you.

Barracuda's Glossary

A

Aboard: On or within the ship or boat.

Accordion: A box-shaped musical instrument that is bellows-driven.

Archipelago: A group of islands.

Arquebus: A "hook gun" or "hook tube"—an early muzzle-loaded firearm used in the 15th-17th centuries.

Artilleryman: The pirate in charge of the weapons (guns and cannons).

B

Barracuda: The captain of the *Southern Cross*; also a large predatory tropical marine fish with large jaws and teeth.

Bellows: A device that produces a strong current of air when its sides are pressed together (as on an accordion).

Billeted: An official order stating that a military member must be provided with room and board (as in a private home).

Black Jet: A black organic rock that forms when pieces of woody material are buried in sediment and coalified. Jet can be cut, carved, and polished to a luster.

Bodega: A wine cellar.

Brandish: To wave or swing something in a threatening manner (such as a weapon).

Bridge: The area from which one navigates (steers) the ship.

C

Cabin: A compartment for passengers or crew.

Cannon: A large gun that shoots heavy metal or stone balls and that was once a common military weapon.

Captain: The person in command of the ship.

Captain's Chambers: The captain's private room or quarters.

Cistern: A tank for storing water.

Clodhopper: A foolish, awkward, or clumsy person.

Cobblestone: Stones frequently used in the pavement of ancient streets.

Coffer: A strongbox or small chest for holding valuables.

Coiling Ropes: To lay a line down in circular turns.

Command Bridge: The room or platform from where the captain issues commands.

Cord: A long, thin flexible rope made from several twisted strands.

Cove: A small sheltered bay.

Crestfallen: Sad and disappointed.

Cretin: A stupid person.

Crow's Nest: A lookout platform or shelter fixed near the top of the mast of a ship.

Cur (Swindling): A surly or cowardly cheater.

Curse: To swear; also to invoke a supernatural power to inflict harm or punishment on someone.

D

Dagger: A short knife with a pointed and edged blade, used as a weapon.

Damsel: A young, unmarried woman.

Davey Jones's Locker: The place at the bottom of the ocean reserved for pirates.

Deck: The floor of the ship; the walking area.

Diphthong: A sound made by combining two vowels; also known as a gliding vowel.

Disembark: To leave a ship.

Dock: A protected water area in which vessels are moored (also referred to as a pier or a wharf).

Docking: To tie up along a pier or wharf.

Doubloon: A Spanish gold coin.

Drop Anchor: Let down the anchor and moor.

Dutch Antilles: A group of six Caribbean islands that were formally Dutch colonial possessions, also known as the Netherlands Antilles.

E

Ebb: A receding current.

Ebony: A black or very dark brown timber from a mainly tropical tree.

Embark: Go on board a ship.

English Armada: A fleet of English warships.

Escudo: A coin historically used in Portugal and Spain and in their colonies.

Estuary: A partially enclosed body of water where freshwater from rivers or streams flow into the ocean.

Eye Patch: A cover worn over an injured or missing eye.

F

Fabrics Merchant: Someone who owns and runs a cloth manufacturing import or export business; also known as a cloth merchant.

Fate: The power that is believed to control what happens in the future.

Feeding the Fish: To vomit over the side of a vessel from seasickness.

Flows: The rise of an ocean tide.

French Detachment: A group of French troops or ships sent away on a separate mission.

Full to Port: Keep the sails full of wind and to the left.

G

Gale: A very strong wind.

Gangplank: A movable plank used as a ramp to board or disembark from a ship or boat.

Gobsmacked: Utterly astonished; astounded.

Grog: A rum drink mixed with water.

Gunpowder: Invented in China, it is a mixture of sulfur, charcoal, and potassium nitrate used to fire cannons.

H

Happy Shipwrecks: A crew of less-than-stellar pirates.

Helm: The wheel or tiller that controls the rudder.

Highest Mast: The tallest mast (vertical pole) on a ship.

High Seas: International waters.

Hook: The metal device used to replace a pirate's lost hand.

Hourglass: A device with two connected glass bulbs containing sand that takes an hour to pass from the upper to the lower bulb.

Hovel: A small, squalid, unpleasant, or simply constructed dwelling.

Hull: The main body of a vessel.

I

Infantry Battalion: A branch of armed forces that fights on foot.

Inlet: A small arm of the sea, a lake, or a river; a cove or a bay.

Inn: An establishment that provides food, drink, and lodging.

J

Jackpot: To suddenly win a large prize, money, or treasure; to hit the jackpot.

Jerky: Meat cut into strips and dried, using salt as a preservative.

K

Keel: The centerline of a boat running from the front (fore) to the back (aft).

Kerchief: A piece of fabric used to cover the head or to tie around the neck.

L

Lad: A young boy.

Land Ahoy: An exclamation announcing the sighting of land from a ship.

Landfall: An arrival at land on a sea journey.

Layabout: A person who habitually does little or no work.

Leave (on): Time permitted to be away from work or military duty.

Legend: A well-known story that is believed by many people but cannot be verified; also a person famous for doing something extremely well.

Lintel: A piece of wood or stone that lies across a door or window and holds the weight of the structure above it.

Loot: The goods that a pirate takes from his enemy.

Looting: The act of plundering and ransacking to obtain treasures.

Lumberjack: A person who cuts down trees.

M

Mackerel: A derogatory term for a pirate; also a large sea fish with a strong taste.

Mainmast: The tallest mast (vertical pole) on a ship.

Mangy Cur: A mean, cowardly person.

Mardi Gras: The last grand celebration before the Catholic season of Lent begins on Ash Wednesday.

Marionette: A puppet controlled from above using wires or strings.

Marquis: A European nobleman ranking above a count and below a duke.

Mast: A vertical pole on a ship that supports sails or rigging.

Mauser: A type of rifle.

Medallion: A large medal.

Memento: An object kept as a reminder or souvenir of a person or event.

Merchant: Someone who buys and sells goods, especially in large amounts.

Mizzen: A fore-and-aft (forward and rear) sail set on the mizzenmast.

Mooring: An arrangement for securing a ship to a mooring pier.

Moor the Ship: To attach a boat to a mooring buoy or post.

Muck: Dirt, rubbish, or waste matter.

Musket: A light gun with a long barrel that is fired from the shoulder.

Mutiny: An open rebellion against those in charge, especially sailors or pirates against the captain of the ship.

N

Newbie: A brand-new pirate.

O

Open Sea: An expanse of sea away from land.

Oxcart: A cart pulled by oxen.

P

Paella: A Spanish dish of rice, saffron, chicken, seafood, etc., cooked and served in a large shallow pan.

Pantry: The compartment of a ship where food is cooked and prepared.

Parchment: A stiff, flat, thin material made from the prepared skin of an animal and used as a durable writing surface in ancient and medieval times.

Peg Leg: An artificial leg, often carved out of wood.

Pier: A loading platform that extends out from the shore.

Pirate: Someone who attacks and steals from a ship at sea.

Pirate Oath: A solemn promise among pirates.

Plunder: To steal things from a place (such as a city or town), especially by force.

Port: The left side of the ship; also where a ship docks.

Powder Keg: A barrel of gunpowder.

Provisions: A supply of food and other things that are needed.

Prow: The forward-most part of a ship's bow that is above the waterline.

Publicans: A person who owns or manages a tavern; the keeper of a pub.

Python: A large heavy-bodied nonvenomous constrictor snake.

Q

Quarrelsome: To bicker; argue.

Quarters: A room on a ship; the captain's quarters.

R

Rigging: The lines and masts on sailing ships.

Rum: An alcoholic liquor distilled from sugar-cane residues or molasses.

S

Saber: A heavy cavalry sword with a curved blade and a single cutting edge.

Sailcloth: A heavy canvas used for sails.

Scourge: A person or thing that causes great trouble or suffering.

Scribe: One who made copies of documents, especially before the invention of printing.

Scruffy: Shabby and untidy or dirty.

Scurvy: A disease resulting from a severe lack of vitamin C.

Seasick: Suffering from sickness or nausea caused by the motion of a ship at sea.

Second in Command: Someone who is ranked second in a group or organization.

Shaman: Someone who is believed to use magic to cure people.

Shiptrap (wretched): A notoriously dangerous area for ships.

Shiver Me Timbers: A pirate exclamation to express shock, surprise, or annoyance.

Short Pistols: A small gun that can be aimed and fired with one hand.

Skirmish: A brief and usually unplanned fight.

Spanish Armada: A Spanish naval invasion force; a fleet of warships.

Spirits: An alcoholic liquor.

Sprog: A brand-new pirate on board a ship for the first time.

Stations: The specific places where pirates perform their assigned duties.

Steer the Boat: To control the direction in which a ship moves.

Stern: The aft (back) part of the ship.

Stocks (replenish): To refill the ship supplies.

Stowaway: A person who secretly boards a ship to travel undetected and without paying.

Swab the Deck: To clean the ship's deck with a mop.

Swindle: Use deception to cheat someone out of money or possessions.

Swindling Cur: A despicable cheater.

Swordsman: A man who fights with a sword.

T

Tailor: One who makes clothes to fit individual customers.

Tarred and Feathered: Smeared with tar and covered with feathers as a punishment.

Tavern: A place that sells alcoholic drinks, like a bar or a pub.

Tomb: A burial chamber.

Tome: A book, especially a large, heavy, scholarly one.

Treasure Map: A pirate map that marks the location of buried treasure or a valuable secret.

U

Unsheathe: Draw or pull out a weapon (like a knife or saber) from its sheathe or covering.

V

Valarian Root: A flowering plant, the root of which is dried and used as an herbal remedy

Vengeance (dish best served cold): An old phrase that means revenge is more satisfying when exacted in cold blood.

Vermin: Wild animals, like rodents, that carry disease.

W

Walk the Plank: The short walk to a watery grave off a plank that extends off the edge of a ship.

Watch Station: Area where crew members are on duty, such as the crow's nest.

Weigh Anchor: Take up anchor on a ship when ready to depart.

Wooden Pajamas: What a pirate "wears" when he sleeps the big sleep; dead.

Wretches: Despicable or good-for-nothing people.